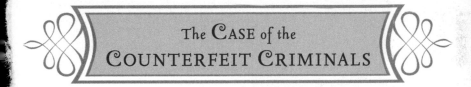

The CASE of the
COUNTERFEIT CRIMINALS

THE WOLLSTONECRAFT
DETECTIVE AGENCY

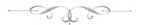

The Case of the Missing Moonstone

The Case of the Girl in Grey

The Case of the Counterfeit Criminals

THE WOLLSTONECRAFT DETECTIVE AGENCY

№ 3

THE CASE OF THE COUNTERFEIT CRIMINALS

JORDAN STRATFORD

ILLUSTRATED BY KELLY MURPHY

ALFRED A. KNOPF NEW YORK

Text copyright © 2017 by Jordan Stratford
Jacket art and interior illustrations copyright © 2017 by Kelly Murphy

All rights reserved. Published in the United States by Alfred A. Knopf, an imprint of Random House Children's Books, a division of Penguin Random House LLC, New York.

Knopf, Borzoi Books, and the colophon are registered trademarks of Penguin Random House LLC.

Visit us on the Web! randomhousekids.com

Educators and librarians, for a variety of teaching tools, visit us at RHTeachersLibrarians.com

Library of Congress Cataloging-in-Publication Data is available upon request.
ISBN 978-0-385-75448-4 (trade) / ISBN 978-0-385-75449-1 (lib. bdg.)
ISBN 978-0-385-75450-7 (ebook)
The text of this book is set in 11.5-point Guardi.

Printed in the United States of America
January 2017
10 9 8 7 6 5 4 3 2 1

First Edition

For Tamsin, Betina, Kelly,
Miki, and Allison

With thanks to Rob Adelson,
Ted and Tara Grand, John Lefebvre,
Nancy Siscoe, Heather Schroder, and Kevin Steil.
And of course to my family,
who puts me up and puts up with me in turn.

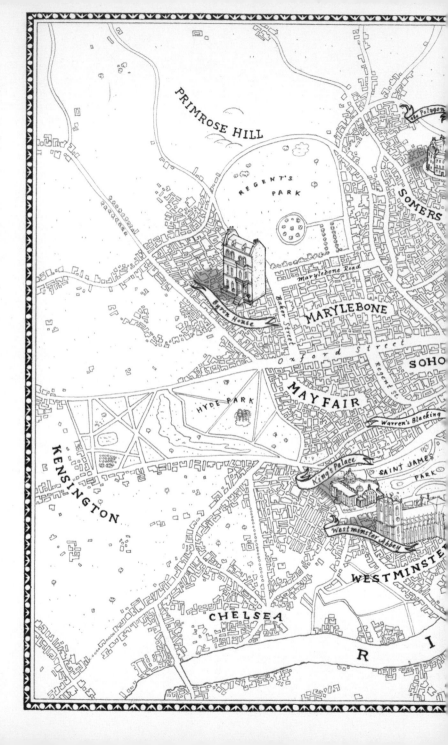

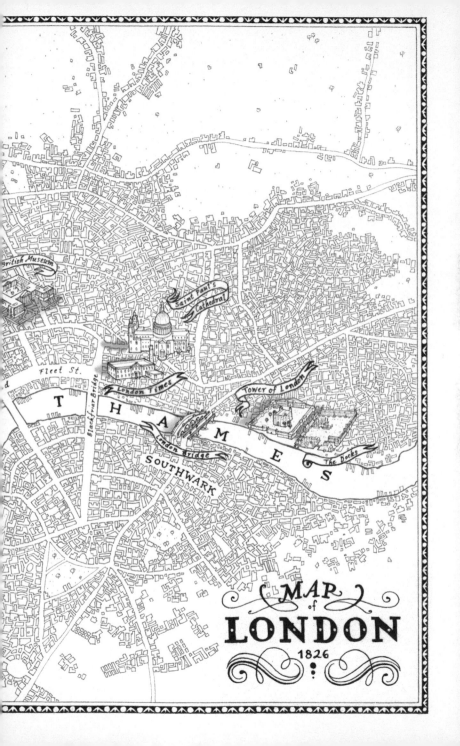

PREFACE

This is a made-up story about two very real girls: Ada Byron, who has been called the world's first computer programmer, and Mary Shelley, the world's first science-fiction author. Ada and Mary didn't really know one another, nor did they have a detective agency together. Mary and Ada were eighteen years apart in age, not three, as they are in the world of Wollstonecraft.

Setting that aside, the characters themselves are as true to history as we are able to tell. At the end of the book, there are notes that reveal more about what happened to each of them in real life, so that you can enjoy the history as much as I hope you'll enjoy the story. Because the history bit is *brilliant.*

—JORDAN STRATFORD

QED

Rain spattered forcefully against Ada's window. The sound merged with the shushing in her ears, mashed as they were against the pillows that propped her up in bed. It was difficult reading only with her right hand, but she was making good progress turning the page with her thumb, though it made her wrist ache. This took her mind away from the wet, black, squirming creatures embedded in her left arm, slowly drinking her blood.

Her book was also a refuge from the stranger who sat at her bedside. The man gave her a chill whenever she thought of him, let alone looked at him, with his pale complexion and dark caterpillar eyebrows.

That's not fair, Ada admitted to herself. Now that she was on the doorstep of her twelfth birthday, she was trying to be more grown-up about this sort of thing. She knew her aversion to strangers, to new things, wasn't entirely rational. And the man was, she supposed, not entirely a stranger, despite his strangeness. Dr. Polidori had been a friend of her father's, the father she scarcely knew. And he'd been there, day after tedious day, draining away her blood in small munching gulps from his little pets—the leeches he would gently pluck away with steel forceps and place in their glass jar when he was done.

"Almost there," said the doctor in his strange, unplaceable accent, as though sensing Ada's discomfort. "We must purge the fevered blood."

"One would think," said Ada, meaning herself, "that someone with no blood would be dead, and someone with blood would be more likely to be alive."

"That is the case, yes," said Dr. Polidori slowly.

"Therefore, more blood is better than less blood, QED," declared Ada. "That's Latin, *quod erat demonstrandum,* meaning 'thus it is proven.'"

"Your Latin is excellent, Lady Ada," the doctor acknowledged distantly, teasing away the leeches with his long steel instrument and dabbing the leftover drops of blood on her arm.

"Mmm," she said. "Then why are you taking blood out of me?"

"You suffered a terrible fever," the doctor declared. "This poisons the blood, which must be removed for you to regain your . . . vitality." He savored the final word in a way that made Ada queasy. But she was often queasy after her leechings.

"Not all my blood, surely," Ada said.

"Merely the fevered blood." Ada again queased at the way he said "blood," like he'd dropped his tongue on a tiled floor, the word easing and then flopping in his mouth.

"How can they tell? The leeches, I mean. How do they know fevered blood from good blood?"

The doctor continued restoring the black worms to their jar. "Such is a mystery of nature."

"It's the sort of thing someone ought to be figuring out."

Polidori said nothing.

"I mean," Ada continued, "there you are, a little

leech, happily lapping up fevered blood, and then you find a spot of perfectly ordinary, good blood. Do you say *Ugh, no thank you, I couldn't possibly*? I don't see it happening. Honestly, there ought to be some sort of evidence. . . ."

Just then, Ada's bedroom door clicked open. Gravity and old hinges let the door drift slowly and ghostlike to the wall of its own accord, and in cartwheeled Ada's nine-year-old half sister, Allegra, still in her nightdress.

The girl thrust her arms above her head in a silent *ta-da!* pose, curls bouncing around her face, until she caught sight of Dr. Polidori.

"Aaaaack!" Allegra said, and hurried out of the room.

"Allegra is not fond of leeches," said Ada to Polidori, who again said nothing.

INTRACTABLES

An hour later, Ada had breakfasted and wiggled wearily into her cherry velvet gown, and made her way to the drawing room in search of a newspaper. She smiled at her best friend, Mary, who stood and gave Ada's hand a squeeze. Mary's stepsister, Jane, stood and gave a halfhearted curtsy. Allegra stayed seated in an overstuffed chair, books at her feet unopened, scone crumbs scattered down her morning dress.

The girls' tutor, Peebs, opened his rain-wet leather case and began extracting books, nodding and smiling at the girls. It was not a particularly talkative morning, how-do-you-dos apparently having been satisfied downstairs, before Ada's arrival.

Despite it being a grand room for a grand house, the sprawl of girls and books and tutor made the drawing room seem almost cramped. Ada, still tired from her daily leeching, retreated behind a grey wall of newsprint to survey the *Times* and see what was going on in the world beyond the stately townhouse in Marylebone.

In truth, Ada was only half-reading, or perhaps reading with half her brain. When the reading half paused to see what the other half had been up to, it continued reading, because what the other half had, in fact, been up to was writing. Ada had written a name in pencil, right there in the pages of the *Times*.

Nora Radel.

Mary Somerville, the smartest woman in the whole world and the Wollstonecraft Detective Agency's last client, had said that Nora Radel was the cleverest girl in all of England.

Which made Ada the second cleverest. And, therefore, the most curious.

Who was this mysterious girl? Why had Ada's friend and mathematical mentor, Mr. Babbage, who reportedly knew this Nora person, never mentioned her before? Exactly how much cleverer was she than Ada herself, and in what way? The whole thing was driving her mad, or would be if she'd had the energy. But the leeches had drained her, so she was mostly just woozy. Despite all her researches, she'd found no trace of Nora Radel.

Down the hall in her room, in the midst of a stack of books Ada could picture perfectly, lay a notebook entitled "Intractables," which contained a series of questions Ada could not pose to her Byron Ligno-tractatic Engine, or "bleh" for short. The bleh was a large brass calculating contraption of her own invention. It could take into account dozens of factors in a problem via a set of spindles and sprockets, and then clack along until a pattern appeared, which Ada would read as a solution. Or at least a different starting point.

The bleh was very good for keeping track of things with numbers, like how often a white horse could be seen in the road between the hours of ten and eleven each morning. It could take in the number of times the newspaper reported burglaries involving portraits, and it could even show relationships between the two sets of numbers (horses and burglaries). Even nun sightings, which Allegra had insisted were worth keeping track of.

But, as yet, the bleh was not particularly good at understanding the patterns of *people*. Such unexpected things she kept track of in her intractables notebook, as there was simply no quantifying them.

Nora Radel was such an intractable. Even though Ada had set a spindle aside for her, there were few variables defined, no way of putting the pegs in the holes that made any sense: Girl, yes. London, yes. Clever, yes. Cleverer than me, (a reluctant) yes. Known to Mr. Babbage and Mrs. Somerville, yes.

Not much to work with.

And, she had to admit, not much reason to care. She'd had little time for the bleh these past weeks. She had a dirt map to finish and a hot-air balloon to rebuild. Yet care she did.

"Kingdom, phylum, class, order, family, genus, species," said Peebs, beginning his lecture. "Keeping precious creatures organized for grumpy scientists," he finished, laughing at his own joke. None of the girls responded in any way.

"Ah," he concluded. "Right, then."

"Taxonomy," said Ada, not looking up from her newspaper.

"Precisely," said Peebs.

"I'm terribly sorry," interjected Mary. "But I haven't a clue as to what you're going on about. Perhaps if—"

"Not a word," interrupted Jane.

"Nope," said Allegra. "Start over."

"Taxonomy," Ada repeated. "It's how you organize animals, how you name them."

"Precisely," said Peebs. "Thank you, Lady Ada. In this way we can categorize all manner of animal in the world—including humans."

"Humans are not animals," snipped Jane.

"I'm afraid we are, Miss Jane," countered Peebs.

"I'm an animal," volunteered Allegra cheerfully.

"Circus chimp," suggested Ada from the recesses of her newspaper.

Peebs rolled his eyes, and Mary was about to intervene when she noticed a number of things in quick succession.

First, through the open door she noticed Mrs. Woolcott, Ada's former governess and current fever-nurse, walking down the corridor, toward the stairs. Next, she noticed Mr. Franklin, Ada's extraordinarily

tall and ever-silent butler, coming up the stairs with what appeared to be an overflowing letters-tray. This was unusual, as the girls had had almost no letters in recent weeks. And, most curiously of all, she noticed a silent exchange between Mrs. Woolcott and Mr. Franklin, in which Mrs. Woolcott offered a very clear "no" with the shake of her head, gathered the bundle of letters, and headed down the hallway toward the library.

When her attention returned to the drawing room, Mary was startled to see Ada staring directly at her.

"What?" said Ada.

"What what, Ada?"

"What you were noticing what, Mary. I notice when you notice things. I'm getting quite good at it."

All eyes were on Mary now.

"Is everything all right, Miss Mary?" Peebs asked.

"I just . . . It seems that . . . Well, I believe there is correspondence," said Mary, uncomfortably on the spot.

"Correspondence," said Ada, folding her newspaper. She looked quickly around the room.

"Library," Ada announced. "Now."

A PURELY THEORETICAL EXERCISE

"Absolutely not," said Mrs. Woolcott.

"Mrs. Woolcott, I'm certain—" Mary began.

"We are all of us certain of precisely one thing, Miss Godwin, and that is that Dr. Polidori has made it very clear that Lady Ada is to be allowed out of bed for meals and brief tutoring only," insisted Mrs. Woolcott. She had turned from clicking the key in a cabinet to spy a gaggle of girls at the library door, insisting on seeing the newly arrived letters.

"Miss Coverlet—" Ada began.

"It is Mrs. Woolcott now, Lady Ada," corrected Mrs. Woolcott.

"Fine. But those are my letters," Ada said crossly.

"Ours, to be perfectly frank," said Jane, and a little whirring click in the counters of Ada's brain noticed that it was a rather rude tone for Jane to be taking.

Ada went to plop herself in her favorite high-backed chair when she stopped suddenly.

"What have you done with my chair?"

"Nothing at all, Lady Ada; it is right there in front of you," Mrs. Woolcott assured.

"It's not. It's got the wrong all everything."

"I had the cushion reupholstered, if that is what you are referring to."

Ada gave it a poke with a finger and made a face.

Mary and Allegra shot each other a she-shouldn't-have-done-that look, thinking of poor Mrs. Woolcott. Everything was silent for the briefest of moments while Ada sucked in all the air from the room.

"MR. FRANKLINNNN!" Ada bellowed.

It was as though he had been standing there the entire time, invisible, and only now materialized. The butler loomed in the doorframe, silent and expressionless.

"I need my chair from the drawing room. And get rid of . . . that." She waved vaguely in the direction of the library chair.

"Please," whispered Mary.

"Please," Ada repeated.

"Mrs. Woolcott," Mary intervened. "Lady Ada will be seated presently, and tucked in with a blanket if you like. Reading her correspondence would hardly be more taxing than undertaking her studies."

"It is not reading the correspondence that concerns me," said Mrs. Woolcott. "It's what comes after. Eavesdropping in thunderstorms. Breaking into hospitals. Running off to crypts at all hours . . ."

"Perhaps," Mary added as Mr. Franklin arrived with the overstuffed and un-reupholstered chair from the drawing room, "if Ada read her mail as a purely theoretical exercise . . ."

"What's 'theoretical'?" asked Allegra.

"Thinking," said Mary, smiling. "A thinking-only sort of exercise. A puzzle to be solved in a very relaxing, sitting-down, not-taking-any-action sort of way."

"That's not quite . . . ," Ada began, having settled in her more-familiar chair.

"Completely uneventful, I assure you, Mrs. Woolcott," finished Mary.

Mrs. Woolcott was unassured, but turned to the small wooden cabinet in which she had locked the neat bundle of letters. After a satisfying click, and a nearly inaudible sigh, the stack was placed in Ada's lap.

Ada struggled for a moment with the string, which was knotted in a precise bow. As she tugged, the knot seemed to grow tighter.

Allegra leapt up from the floor, where she had settled, and neatly sliced the string with a penknife. Ada looked at her little sister in surprise, and was going to ask where the knife had come from, but just as quickly the blade disappeared as though it had never been there in the first place. Proud of herself, Allegra gave a quick smile and sat back down.

"I daresay, we ought to cancel that advertisement in the *Times*," said Mary. "I'd completely forgotten."

"Oh, Charles did that, ages ago," said Ada.

"He did?" asked Mary. Charles was the boy who shared her morning carriage rides, always with his nose in a book, and he had frequently aided the detectives when needed. Mary felt put out, as making requests of Charles generally fell to her, and she knew nothing of this one.

"Peebs's idea," Ada said, which helped Mary's feelings a little.

"Missives are still arriving, though," remarked Jane. "Word of your problem-solving prowess has spread, I fear, Ada."

Mrs. Woolcott, with an additional yet futile sigh and possibly a slight rolling of the eyes, retired from the library, closing the door behind her.

Ada glanced at the missives and began firing unopened letters at Mary, Jane, and Allegra in turn. The girls began to pop open the wax seals and scan the contents.

"Dates," said Ada almost immediately. "Dates, dates, dates."

"What's wrong, Lady Ada?" asked Jane.

"We haven't had a Wollstonecraft letter for weeks. Then this stack, from yesterday and this morning," Ada said.

"So?" asked Allegra.

"So, it's wrong. If this were a random sampling,

we'd see nothing, and then something. Something is always caused by something else. And nothing's happened. It's been dull as ditchwater around here."

"So?" asked Allegra again.

"So, this is not a random increase in messages. It's not an increase at all," Ada declared. "MRS. WOOLCOTT!" Ada roared.

The girls could hear the steps down the hall, and the library door opened. Mrs. Woolcott appeared with a large market basket overflowing with letters, all in bundles, and tied with string. "I assumed you'd want these as well," she said.

Allegra set to work at once, snicking open the bundles with her magically appearing and disappearing penknife, and flinging the letters at different girls as though she were dealing cards.

"Allegra! I had a system!" objected Ada. Allegra shrugged, already reading a letter, and pulling a face.

"What's wrong?" whispered Jane.

"I can't read this handwriting," said Allegra.

"Here, we'll switch," Jane offered.

"I had a system!" Ada insisted.

And so they began. Each girl would read, in turn, the first few lines of the letters, each asking for help

from the Wollstonecraft Detective Agency. Ada would answer each with a sharp "no" or a bored "no" or a pained and frustrated "no."

"Dear—" Mary began.

"No," clipped Ada.

"Ada, you can't possibly—"

"Can. No."

"After a 'Dear'?" said Mary, bewildered.

"You read it funny," said Ada.

It was Jane's turn, but she wasn't reading aloud.

"Jane?" prodded Mary.

"Well, you won't like this one, Ada. It's just about a missing dog."

"Where?" asked Ada, suddenly alert.

"Lyme Regis, in Dorset," replied Jane.

Allegra piped in. "That's miles away."

"Terrier?" asked Ada.

"What's that?" asked Allegra.

"Terrier. Dog. Animalia, *Chordata, Mammalia, Carnivora, Canidae, Canis, Canis lupus, Canis lupus familiaris.* Yappy rectangular things. Eyebrows."

"Why, yes, Ada, how did you—" Jane began.

"This one. We take the dog case." Ada held out her hand, and Jane relinquished the letter.

Mary knew better than to press further, but Jane and Allegra did not.

But before they were able to extract any kind of explanation as to why this particular case, they could hear a great flurry of activity downstairs. There was no knock, just the door downstairs and the sound of footmen and luggage and rushing and other such goings-on.

The library door reopened, and a shocked-looking Mrs. Woolcott entered.

"Allegra," she said, "come with me. Now."

"Whatever is the—" Jane began.

Mrs. Woolcott interrupted her, pale and serious. "Allegra. Servants' stairs. Now. Quick quick."

Allegra looked frightened, but Ada trusted Mrs. Woolcott and gave her little sister a reassuring nod.

"Go," Ada said.

"You two," instructed Mrs. Woolcott to Jane and Mary, "remain in the library, door closed. Silently. Into the bleh closet if you must," she said, pointing to the half-open door to the room that housed Ada's tall brass contraption. "Anna will come fetch you when it's safe. Ada, bed, now, silent as dust. Do you understand?"

THE OSTRICH
AND THE PUG

Christmas, Ada thought. *We were supposed to have until Christmas.*

Ada kicked her slippers under the bed and hopped in, pulling the blankets up to hide her cherry dress. She tucked the missing-dog letter under her pillow for safekeeping. There was a clatter of activity in the hall, and she knew, knew in what was supposed to be her fevered blood, that that kind of clatter could only come in the churning wake of her battleship of a mother.

The baroness had long ago left her daughter Ada

Each girl nodded. Allegra took Mrs. Woolcott's hand and disappeared down the hall to a narrow door that might be mistaken for a cupboard. Ada knew well the narrow and creaking stairs that led to the back kitchen and pantry, although with no adults in the house, the servants had become accustomed to using the main stairs.

Ada gave a last, wide-eyed look at Mary, mouthed "hide the letters," then clicked the library door behind her.

to the care of the servants of the Marylebone house, with the strict instruction that none of Ada's father's former associates—with the exception of leechy Dr. Polidori—were to be admitted. Peebs had flouted this rule by applying for the job of her tutor using a clandestine name, so that he might keep an eye on the daughter of his deceased friend. For Ada's father, Lord Byron, and Peebs had indeed been the best of friends, as close as Mary was to Ada. The baroness had tried to fire him, but she wasn't in London, and Peebs was. Until now.

The baroness hadn't left Ada on purpose, really. It was more that the baroness hated the Marylebone house as much as Ada hated change. So while her mother felt she must go, Ada felt she must stay. She wasn't alone. There was Mr. Franklin, her butler; Miss-Coverlet-now-Mrs.-Woolcott, her former governess; Anna the maid; and Mrs. Chowder—Chowser, Ada corrected herself—the cook. All the other servants—footmen, maids, and scullions—were trundled off to Kirkby Mallory, in Leicestershire. And they were to remain, with all their great many names, at least until Christmas, which was still some weeks away.

But the clamor of unpacking and unbundling could only mean one thing: the return of the baroness to Marylebone.

A begloved and bewigged footman swung Ada's door open, clacked his heels together, and gave an almost mechanical nod. In sailed a woman who always reminded Ada of an ostrich. Right now, an ostrich bearing a wheezing, flat-faced, and snotty pug.

"Gran?" said Ada—to the ostrich, not the pug.

"Good heavens, child. It is as I feared. You're scarcely alive," said Gran.

"I'm fine, honestly," said Ada quietly. "Except for all the leeches."

"Leeches. Of course. Best thing for fever. But I can hardly expect a mere child to have a grasp of such things. And your room! How dreadfully unbecoming for a young lady." Ada's gran, the Honorable Lady Judith Noel, scanned the room, with its grease-stained carpet, and little tumbleweeds of crumpled paper, and bits and bobs of brass gears, and dissected toys.

"I am not a mere child," objected Ada, strongly.

"Now, now. Do not excite yourself. No doubt that is what attracted the fever. Excitement."

"I was caught in a storm," Ada tried to explain.

"Nonsense, child. There is no way you could possibly be exposed to anything so dangerous as a storm. You're a little girl."

Ada was about to add that the storm had merely been an inconvenience while she was eavesdropping on rather cruel and horrid criminals, but thought better of it.

Gran put the pug down, who began snarfling the carpet, leaving little shiny trails of snot wherever it sniffed. As it waddled hurriedly to the corner of the room where Ada had carefully arranged a number of shallow jars of collected soil, the creature's bloated sausage of a body knocked over several specimens, rolling them all out of order.

"My dirt map!" exclaimed Ada, nearly jumping out of bed.

"Dirt? How revolting. We shall have those disposed of at once. Charlemagne!" Lady Noel called to the pug. "Charlemagne, be a good boy."

The dog's black squashed face attempted to smile, but its tongue fell out instead. Its little pig tail did almost seem to wag, although Ada could not tell if the animal was happy or if it just really had to go to the bathroom.

"Well, and here you are, without so much as a companion," Gran said to Ada (she hoped) and not to Charlemagne.

"But I do have a companion," said Ada. "Mary—"

"Oh, I know all about that detective agency nonsense, and that Godwin girl. No, dear, I mean someone of your station. A young lady of breeding. Your cousin Libby, perhaps."

Ada was confused, but Gran's prattle bore the unpleasant odor of "Society," so she did not ask for clarification.

"Mary is my friend," said Ada, perhaps more rudely than she had intended. "And that's that."

"Headstrong. You've always been headstrong," mused Gran.

"She's here," said Ada. "Now. In the library." All of this was becoming too much for Ada—Mrs. Woolcott keeping her letters from her, the mis-sorting of cases, Jane acting strangely, though Ada didn't understand exactly how or why, but thought she ought to.

"Is she, indeed?" Gran raised an eyebrow and shot a look at the footman, who nodded and slipped out.

Gran scooped up the wheezing bottle-cork of a

dog and looked around her with obvious distaste. She waited.

Mary peeked in the doorway, the footman immediately behind her.

"Ada?" Mary asked, to see if her friend was all right.

"Miss Godwin, I presume," said Gran, looking Mary over.

"Lady Byron, I'm very pleased to make your acquaintance," answered Mary with her best curtsy.

"Good heavens, child, do you mistake me for my own daughter?" laughed Gran. "Oh, you flatterer, you. It shall get you nowhere, though." Clearly, she was pleased. "Now, then, let's have a look at you." And she reached out to Mary's chin with thumb and forefinger, turning Mary's jaw gently to the light, as though she were buying a horse. Charlemagne wheezed and snortled at Mary, seemingly in approval. "Aren't you a dear. Given a proper match, you could have the world on a pin."

"You should rest, child," Gran said to Ada, but with a meaningful look at Mary. This was a woman who expected to be obeyed.

With that, the odd ostrich of a woman brushed

past Mary and strode from the room, her footman falling in behind.

Mary shut the door after her.

"So, that was not your mother?" Mary asked, still a little overwhelmed.

"Grandmother."

"Well," said Mary, looking for something positive to say. "Does that mean that Allegra can come out of hiding?"

"No," said Ada with a sigh. "Intractable."

GASLIGHT

5

Allegra paced in the white upstairs kitchen. At least, that's what Ada had always called it, but it was really a butler's pantry, with a back door to the garden for deliveries, and the distillery closet in which the girls had locked Peebs in their first adventure together.

It was also a ready source for bread and butter. Ada was in the habit of wandering in and helping herself, as opposed to asking the servants for it, and Allegra had followed suit. The real kitchen was downstairs, at the end of the dim hall where Allegra knew the servants lived, and where a small army of unmet servants were currently installing themselves—more at home here than she was herself.

This will require some sneaking, Allegra thought.

The nine-year-old had perfected her sneaking skills in whisper-quiet convents on the Continent, where she'd lived most of her life. And she'd successfully sneaked away from the latest convent altogether to come here and be a Wollstonecraft detective with Ada. Allegra and Ada shared the same father, but not the same mother, and the baroness was likely to explode if she found Allegra here. When the baroness had been far away in the country, that prospect had seemed almost amusing. With the baroness perhaps only a few steps away from her current hiding place, Allegra decided sneaking was the better option and slipped through the door and headed down the stairs.

This was a relatively easy sneak: the bustling and noise of the movers-in covered the sound of her footsteps. She saw the lean backs of footmen in wigs and maids in caps bending, folding, lifting, sorting, and unpacking, the rooms filling up with trunks and bags and bundles. A room for every one of them. And not a single room, Allegra knew, for her.

At one end of the hall was the kitchen proper,

which Allegra knew well enough to avoid. There, her discovery would be certain. At the other end of the hall was a great green door, one that had always been locked. But now, amazingly, a key protruded from the keyhole.

Allegra pressed herself to the wall and slowed her breathing. With her eyes, she counted the steps to the beckoning door and watched the fluttering of shadows in the doorframes to the servants' rooms. She waited for what seemed like hours but was, she knew, only about a dozen heartbeats. She was good at this. She smiled.

Then perfectly naturally, her timing everything, Allegra strode unhurried down the long corridor to her great green prize and turned the key. Its heavy click was masked by the clamor of pots and pans in the kitchen, and the creak of the hinges was drowned out by that of other doors and cupboards.

Allegra stepped in and closed the door behind her. For a minute her heart pounded—a reminder that she should have brought the key with her, that someone might turn the key and lock her in, there, in the dark. She shrugged at the thought. She'd find a way out.

It was not completely dark. Gas lamps in sconces along the brick walls were turned almost all the way down, lighting the top stairs, with the rest falling into the gloom. But a small brass key, like the windup on the back of a marching doll, was set into the brick, and a half turn woke all the flames up.

There was light enough to show the way. At the bottom of the rough wooden stairs waited another stout oak door, with an old-fashioned iron ring for a handle. Behind that (and Allegra was slightly disappointed to find that bats did not fly out of the darkness when she opened it) was a stone stairwell, and at the bottom, a forgotten secret laboratory.

Allegra turned up the gaslights. Before her were hefty oaken tables, longer than any she had ever seen, a stone floor swept recently, and relatively organized and squared-away stacks of papers. There were bins for mechanical parts, and gears sorted by size, and neat bundles of wire in copper and brass. Iron tools hung from the wall. Jars containing specimens, concoctions, and potions, which, on closer inspection, proved to be salts, crystals, and acids, all labeled first in a hurried scrawl and then again in a more patient hand—presumably Ada's and then Mrs. Woolcott's.

There were blueprints, and tables of mathematical calculations, and a sketch of blocks, and pipes, and something that looked like the inner workings of the ratcheting spindles of a music box. Allegra's fingers dusted the paper.

"It's the bleh," she said aloud in amazement.

"This is where she built it. Or the parts of it," came Mrs. Woolcott's voice behind her.

Allegra nearly jumped out of her skin. Mrs. Woolcott was clearly an expert sneaker herself.

"I cleaned out the back room of the library for it," Mrs. Woolcott continued, "or she never would have come upstairs."

Allegra walked over to a new-looking crate, which sat on a platform connected to the ceiling by heavy chains. Craning her neck, she could make out a thin slit of daylight through an iron door in the ceiling.

"It's a trapdoor, and an elevator; it opens in the side garden. The crate contains Mr., er, Peebs's gift to Ada. A steam engine, for a new balloon, I believe. I daresay she's been in no condition to think about that project."

Allegra continued to poke about the laboratory in awe. It spanned the entire footprint of the Marylebone house, and beyond. There was a pile of crates in a far, unlit corner and a hint of an archway in stone behind.

"Are those . . . tunnels?"

Mrs. Woolcott stood patiently in the eerie gaslight. "Allegra, it's time to go."

Allegra suddenly felt very small, and very much alone there in the cold stone room. She was reminded of the day she had taken her small bundle of things, some Italian and English money her father had given her long ago, which she had hidden from the other orphans in the convent, and set out in search of this very house. In hopes of a home.

Mrs. Woolcott extended a gloved hand, and a kindly smile.

"Dear Allegra. Time for a new adventure."

Less than a minute later, holding hands, Mrs. Woolcott and Allegra hurriedly crossed the threshold of the upstairs-kitchen delivery door into the garden of the Byron house in Marylebone, and then passed through the garden gate to the gravel alley and into the vast bustle of London beyond.

Alone in the library, Jane took stock of her situation.

She had often imagined herself lounging alone in a stately home such as this, with a bell rope in the corner just like that one over there, with which to summon servants. Tea or cakes or whatever she fancied—with a pull of the rope, it would be brought to her.

I could pull that rope now, if I wanted, she thought.

But she had no right to, not really. This was not her home, and these were not her servants. And after the revelations of foul play in their last case—by supposed gentlemen! Well, even though she was only twelve, Jane had glimpsed enough of Society proper to see that entitlement and merit were not as connected as she had first assumed. She could pull that rope, and someone would have to stop whatever they were doing, and climb the long stairs up to the library, just to see what she wanted, and then go back down and fetch it and bring it up again. All because of the pull of a bell rope. She hardly thought it fair, and her heart was heavier for it.

Jane opened the library door. Her chin high, she walked down the hall, ignoring the servants but casting a glance into Ada's room as she passed. She saw Mary's curtsy and an elderly woman, who Jane thought must be the baroness, smile and nod at Mary approvingly.

Acceptance. That's what she saw. Jane felt as though she were carved from wood.

She made her way down the stairs to the foyer, where Mr. Franklin stood and watched her descend. Over his arm were her cape and bonnet and gloves, all of which looked suddenly plain and worn thin, there in the gleaming white hall. She told herself not to cry, and succeeded, at least for the moment.

Mr. Franklin, as impossibly tall and silent as always, helped her with her cape as she buttoned the wrists of her gloves. With a nod and what almost, in certain lights, might resemble a small smile, he opened the front door of the shining Byron house, onto Marylebone Road.

What Jane saw made her breath catch in her throat.

Dolls, or mannequins, she thought at first. But no, people. People painted to look like dolls, round rosy cheeks and all. One man, and one woman. Even from across the broad road, she could see lines drawn around their wrists, around finger joints, as though they had been meticulously assembled.

They had frozen in place upon realizing they'd

been spotted, which made the whole scene even more bizarre. Jane simply had no place in her brain in which to put such a sight.

Just then, a monstrous omnibus drove past, and in its trembling wake the mysterious doll figures had completely vanished.

Jane hopped back into the house, her eyes wide, her mouth agape. She looked to her left at Mr. Franklin, who had clearly not caught sight of the strangely painted couple, or if he had, he was unaffected by it. She looked to her right and saw Peebs in the parlor, tucking the last of his papers and books into his leather case, making to leave.

"Peebs?" Jane asked.

Peebs looked up and caught the expression of shock on Jane's face.

"Are you all right, Miss Jane?" he asked, concerned.

"I just saw . . . well, I don't know what I saw. It's all a bit much, I'm afraid."

"Certainly many changes are afoot, Miss Jane. But we must persevere, in our way."

"I confess I cannot see a way through it at all, what with Ada's mother having returned."

"Grandmother, actually," clarified Peebs. "I suspect the baroness is still some weeks away, if ever she should decide to return. However, it is best, I think, if we all give the situation a degree of remove."

"But we've just found a new case! A missing dog, in Dorset."

"Well, under the watchful gaze of Lady Noel, I do not expect Lady Ada to be allowed out of the house. I fear the unfortunate dog shall have to remain missing."

Jane was frustrated. "Lady this and Lady that. It's all right for you. You're one of them."

"Miss Jane," clarified Peebs patiently. "I am one of my own, thank you. And while I certainly understand your frustrations at some aspects of Society—indeed, I share them—we can be of little help to Ada by remaining here. If we are to be of service, and I suspect we shall be needed, then we must adopt a manner more clandestine."

Jane tried harder not to cry, and it was almost working.

"There, there, Miss Jane. I am certain all will be well. We have faced greater challenges than an obstructive grandmother!"

Jane merely nodded before asking, "Peebs, might I perhaps trouble you for carriage fare home?"

"Certainly, Miss Jane. I shall escort you, if you like."

"If it's all the same, I'd rather go alone," Jane said bravely.

"You know, that's considered not at all proper," Peebs said with a slight smile.

"I know," said Jane.

"I may as well be in Newgate," said Ada. "Only with leeches."

"I'm sure it won't be as bad as all that," said Mary assuringly.

"Gran won't let me near a door, let alone through it—you'll see."

"We've managed to sneak out before. We'll think of something."

"Or not," said Ada.

"Whatever do you mean?" asked Mary.

"I have things to do. Important things."

"Like the missing dog," added Mary.

"Yes. No. I mean *my* things. Important things." Ada pointed to the jars on the floor. "I have a dirt map to organize. I have the bleh to program with Mr. Babbage. There are books I haven't read yet. And I have a dozen seamstresses to manage."

"Seamstresses?" Mary asked.

"I'm just—I don't know. It's all gone wrong. Jane knows."

"Yes, I must admit my sister does not seem quite herself."

"We broke her, I think," Ada declared.

The door opened, and it was Anna, Ada's maid.

"Sorry to intrude, Lady Ada. I just thought you should know that they've all gone."

"My gran and her servants?" Ada asked.

"No. Miss Jane, Miss Allegra, Mrs. Woolcott, and Mr. Peebs."

"Where did they go?"

"Home for Jane. Home too for Allegra and Mrs. Woolcott; I mean to say, Mrs. Woolcott's taken Allegra to her home. And I'm not sure as to Mr. Peebs's whereabouts, only that he has left."

"Mmm." Ada pursed her lips sourly.

Anna nodded and stepped backward through the door, closing it.

"That's that, then," Ada said after a moment.

"Honestly, Ada, I'm sure that—" Mary began.

"Well, I'm not. It's impossible. And just as well."

Even the air between the girls felt hurtful to Mary.

"You can't just give up like this," said Mary quietly.

"Can," replied Ada, her face stiffening.

"I see," said Mary as calmly as she could manage, which wasn't very. She rose from Ada's bed, where she had been perched, and gave a resigned, heartbroken sigh.

"No," said Ada, quite loudly.

"No what, Ada?"

"No, you don't just stand up and say you see when you don't. I get . . . stuck, sometimes. And you get me unstuck. It's what you do."

"So, you want me to unstick you?" asked Mary tentatively.

Ada nodded. "Go on, then."

"Well, all right. We may be scattered, but we are not lost to each other. And we have a case to attend to. So put your mind to that. I can write to this address in . . ."

"Lyme Regis, Dorset."

"Yes, and inquire about the missing dog."

"London to Dorset, one hundred fifty-four miles."

"Really? You are a marvel, Ada," acknowledged Mary.

"I like maps. They stay put," said Ada. "Anyway, that's three days there, three days back by post. And another two days for the carriage. So we shall expect Miss Mary Anning of the missing-terrier case to arrive a week from tomorrow." Ada handed Mary the letter, which Ada had tucked under her pillow.

"However shall we get her into the house?" Mary wondered.

"It would certainly help if there was a secret elevator from the street through the side garden that descended into some sort of underground catacomb that Gran doesn't know about."

Mary scanned her friend's expression to see if there was any clue she was joking.

There was none.

THOUSANDS OF THOUSANDS

December sent a calling card in the form of an icy blob of rain down the back of Allegra's neck, but the girl did not care at all. In fact, she was blissfully happy.

Happy to have received Ada's message, after a week, instructing her to return discreetly to Marylebone and help with the case. Happy that Mrs. Woolcott and her husband, Cecil, were trying to make a home for her in their modest flat. Happy even to just be outside, in the rain.

Her happiness was jolted when she spotted something across the street from the Byron house as comical as it was disturbing. Two clowns (she supposed) in white powder, with perfectly round red circles on their cheeks. Not clowns, she thought. Dolls. Puppets?

Little lines ran around their visible joints, including an uncomfortable-looking one under the jaw. As if their heads might pop off any minute.

She was distracted by the arrival of a carriage and a youngish-not-oldish woman with rather a great deal of luggage. She was insisting "gently, please, gently" as the coachman handed it down.

Miss Mary Anning, of Lyme Regis, Dorset. Had to be. And with her arrival, the disappearance of the curious doll couple.

Allegra glanced at the still-closed door of the Marylebone house, stepped behind a crisply rectangular hedge, and whistled. It was a rather extraordinary whistle, produced with two fingers in the little girl's mouth, and it made the horses snap their ears up. Fortunately, the whistle also gained the attention of Miss Anning's ears, and the ears turned her entire face in Allegra's direction.

Allegra beckoned, and Miss Anning hoisted her various bags and trundled over. Allegra put a finger to her lips in the universal sign for "shhhh" and then pointed to a long black rectangle in the ground at her feet, there in the side garden. Allegra knelt down to rap on the black metal door. Five times.

With a squeak, the steel door split at the middle and opened upward. There was a series of ticks, followed by a rattle of chains, as a rough wooden platform slowly rose up out of the dark, eventually coming level with the grass.

"This way," whispered Allegra as she stepped onto the platform. Miss Anning nodded, stacked her luggage carefully on the platform, and stepped on herself. Allegra did a little hop-step, which reverberated across the wooden deck, and the clicking and rattling resumed, this time carrying the passengers down into inky blackness. The rain continued to write little "how-do-you-dos" on Allegra, who really should have remembered to wear a hat.

Miss Anning could see she was in a vaulted stone room, lit only by gaslights. The room held long, stout wooden tables and piles of tools and metallic things she could not immediately identify. And sitting at one of these tables were two young girls.

"Jane?" Allegra asked. Mary shook her head sadly.

"I suppose you're wondering," Ada began, as she had rehearsed, "why we are meeting underground."

"Not really, to be honest," Miss Anning replied. "Since little Tray disappeared, I've had all sorts of unusual meetings." Ada concealed her disappointment. Nobody ever wondered anything.

"Please, do have a seat, Miss Anning," said Mary, rising, but not figuring out an easy way around the long table. "Oh, it is Miss Anning, I presume?"

"Miss Mary Anning, at your service," the woman said, with a small curtsy. There were no chairs to speak of, but she managed with a wooden stool easily enough.

Miss Anning had an oval face and a soft chin. Her sharp brown eyes sparkled with intelligence, and her nose, while prominent, was long and noble. It was a serious yet kindly face, beneath a very practical straw hat, which Ada decided would be ideal for fossil hunting.

"I'm Mary Godwin," said Mary. "And this is of course Lady Ada Byron, and I see you have already met her half sister, Allegra."

Allegra ignored the introductions and was poking

at the stacks of luggage, though it was too dim to discern much from them.

"Do you know a Nora Radel?" Ada asked out of nowhere. The question had been a wasp in the jar of Ada's brain, and she needed to let it out.

"No, I'm sorry," said Miss Anning. "Should I?"

"Unusual meetings, you were saying," resumed Ada.

"Well, yes, as I said, ever since my poor dog went missing."

"Missing?" asked Ada. "Or dead?"

"Ada!" exclaimed Mary. "That's a horrid thing to say!"

"No," interjected Miss Anning. "It is certainly what I thought at first."

"The landslide," said Ada.

"What landslide?" asked Allegra. "Nobody said anything about a landslide."

"Perhaps," suggested Mary, "we might begin at the beginning."

"Very well," agreed Miss Anning. "As you may know, my family business consists of collecting and selling certain natural antiquities."

"What's natural antiquities?" asked Allegra. Ada

shot daggers at her with a look, but Allegra wrinkled her nose and deflected the imaginary daggers with imaginary steel gauntlets.

"Very old specimens of once-living things," answered Miss Anning helpfully.

"So, dead things," said Allegra.

"Very dead, yes. Very long-dead things. My home in Dorset has the proper geology and weather to expose the remains of animals who have been dead for thousands of thousands of years."

"How can there be thousands of thousands?" Allegra asked.

Ada, if she'd had the energy, would have leapt over the table to throttle her sister. She settled for another deadly stare.

"That is a very reasonable question, Miss Allegra," said Miss Anning. "Tell me, how long does it take you to count to one hundred?"

"Twenty-four seconds," said Ada precisely.

"Indeed, Lady Ada, an impressive yet reasonable sum. Therefore, counting aloud to one thousand, without stopping, would consume approximately four minutes' time."

Allegra shrugged.

"Ah, but if you were to count out loud to a thousand thousand," continued Miss Anning, "which we call a million, it would take you more than two days solid."

"Two days of counting! What if you were thirsty, or had to go to the bathroom, or got bored?" Allegra asked.

"Then either it would take you longer or you would have to have a friend take over," Miss Anning explained. "Of course, I understand that Lady Ada's contraption can count rather a great deal quicker than that."

Ada nodded, pleased.

"Four hours, twenty-seven minutes," said Ada. "But it'll throw a spindle. Best to do it by tens, anyway. Or hundreds. Faster."

"No doubt, Lady Ada. However, to answer your question, Miss Allegra, where my family lives it is quite common to find the bones or even entire skeletons of these ancient animals, thousands of thousands of years old, some of which are very large indeed. We locate, extract, classify, and find scientific homes for these materials, these very old animal bones, so that they may be studied and tell us more about the world as it once was."

"Like this," said Ada. She slid forward a modest-sized framed engraving. In the picture, giant palm trees graced the land, while monstrous animals that resembled fish and crocodiles swam the seas and lined the shore, while giant bat creatures flew overhead.

"Yes, this is a drawing by a friend of mine, Mr. De la Beche. It shows the animals native to Dorset during the Jurassic Period, some millions of years ago."

"Days of counting without sleeping or having to pee," said Allegra.

"As you say," said Miss Anning. "And rather more than that."

"Gosh" was all Mary could say.

Allegra pointed to the print. "So, these sea monsters ate your dog?"

"No, Miss Allegra. Tray—my little dog—and I were exploring a cliff face, which seasonally erodes to reveal some extraordinary specimens, but there was—"

"A landslide. It was in the *Times*," said Ada.

"Aha!" exclaimed Mary. Now she finally understood why Ada had taken such a seemingly mundane case as a missing dog, and one so far from London.

"A landslide, yes. I nearly fell to my death. And, in the aftermath, I was unable to find—"

"Your dog, Tray, the terrier," said Allegra. "See? I was listening."

"Very good, yes," continued Miss Anning. "And so I assumed the worst."

"But the dog isn't dead," said Ada.

"Well," said Miss Anning. "Immediately upon arriving home, and distraught from my fruitless search . . ."

"Should have brought an apple," laughed Allegra, inappropriately. Ada fired her a look, which put a stopper in the outburst.

". . . I discovered a note," continued Miss Anning. "Here." And from her jacket pocket she produced a folded piece of brown paper, sliding it along the wooden workbench to Ada, who picked it up and sniffed it deeply.

"Fishy?" asked Mary.

"A little," Ada answered. "Different, though. Beefy."

"It's butcher paper," said Miss Anning. "Common enough in Dorset, as it's waterproof. We use it to line shelves, patch roof holes. It's quite useful."

"Common doesn't help us. We need uncommon." Ada unfolded the paper and at once understood the beefy smell.

Glue.

Each letter in the note had been clipped from a newspaper and glued onto the waxy brown butcher paper.

It read:

"And where did you find this note?" asked Ada.

"It was on my kitchen table, when I arrived home," Miss Anning explained.

"No sign of forced entry?" asked Ada.

"Lady Ada, I live in Dorset. Our doors do not have locks, for the most part."

"Ah," she said.

"And to what does this refer?" asked Mary. "Lot two twenty-one B, Brit Mus?"

"British Museum," Ada answered. "They're building a new one—a bigger one—and are currently acquiring artifacts for the new collection. It is the largest construction site in all of Europe. Not far from here, actually; you can hear the hammering from the roof."

Mary suddenly felt a pang of sadness for her friend. A hot-air balloon tethered to the roof had been Ada's favorite hideout, but it had been destroyed during their first case. She could tell from the sigh in her voice that Ada must miss it rather dreadfully. Still, she persevered with the matter at hand. "But why would they ask Miss Anning to verify the artifacts?"

"I can guess," said Ada. "One, because they're fake, and two, because Miss Anning is clever enough to say so."

"Thank you for your confidence, Lady Ada," said Miss Anning politely. "And, yes, I suspect they are indeed fake. The lot has been professionally illustrated, and while I have not examined the specimen itself . . ."

"Specimen of what?" asked Allegra.

"It purports to be an intact ichthyosaur skeleton. A marine predator of the late Cretaceous Period," explained Miss Anning.

"A sea monster," said Allegra, nodding.

"A sea monster," Miss Anning agreed. "Although, in this case, I imagine it's a dolphin spine, seal flippers, a crocodile skull, and no small amount of paint and plaster."

"It's a fake?" Allegra asked.

"It certainly appears so from the drawing. I've been asked to verify and authenticate several pieces for the upcoming acquisition, Lot two twenty-one B included. Someone must have known that. As you see from my luggage, I have brought several specimens of my own to sell to the museum while I'm here. But nothing so grand as a complete ichthyosaur skeleton, counterfeit or no."

"Tell me, Miss Anning, you mentioned unusual meetings," Ada said.

"Yes. I received another message, this one from a young boy, a street urchin, I daresay, telling me to meet these 'Sons of Bavaria' on Learn Road. I had never heard of such an organization, nor even such a road in Dorset, and could not locate it on any map. So I was at a loss for how to respond. But while I was in line at the shops, I had the feeling that I was being watched, and sure enough, a large bearded man approached me and said, 'Verify and authenticate,' and then he left."

"Sons of Bavaria . . . ," Ada mused. "Accent?" she asked.

"None to speak of," Miss Anning answered.

"Bavaria is German. You'd think he'd sound German. Describe him," said Ada.

"The fellow was tall, perhaps in his mid-thirties, and bearded. A bit scruffy," explained Miss Anning.

"Sons of Bavaria . . . ," Ada muttered. "Sons of Bavaria. S.O.B. The *S* tattoo!" Ada was thinking back to their two previous cases. One involved a necklace stolen by means of hypnotism, and the other concerned an heiress nearly tricked into marriage by a scoundrel. Totally unrelated cases, and yet there was one connection: an inked letter *S* on the forearms of both villains. There was more to the tattoos, but that was all Ada had been able to make out. . . . Perhaps the rest was O.B.?

Mary gave Ada an inquisitive look.

"Tattoo? Right forearm?" Ada asked Miss Anning.

"No, I'm quite certain. His sleeves were rolled up,

and he wore an apron, like a grocer, and I did not see any tattoos."

"So he was a grocer?" Allegra asked, confused.

"I don't know for sure," admitted Miss Anning. "He could have had any number of reasons to have his sleeves rolled up."

"Including showing you that he had no tattoo!" declared Ada.

Everyone looked around the room, more than a tad confused.

"I'm afraid that doesn't make much sense," admitted Mary quietly.

"Not yet," Ada agreed, feeling a little uncomfortable at her own certainty, based on so little evidence. Indeed, the absence of evidence. "No matter," she said, returning to the case at hand. "We need merely find the Sons of Bavaria, find the dog, reveal the ichthyosaur bones to be counterfeit, and keep Miss Anning's scientific integrity from being compromised. Simple enough," summed up Ada.

"All right, then!" said Mary, squaring her shoulders. "And when is the acquisition, Miss Anning? How long do we have?"

"Three days," replied the burdened scientist. "The acquisition is in three days."

"Ah." Mary drooped.

Miss Anning left them her address at the Golden Alder Inn, promising to be in touch should she hear more from the dognappers. Then she and Allegra returned up the elevator, leaving Mary and Ada alone in the gloom.

"My tummy's funny," said Ada.

"You must be exhausted. It's your first venture out of bed in some time."

"No, it's—I'm not sure. Which is to say I am sure, but I shouldn't be. About the *S* tattoo, I mean."

Mary nodded. "You have a hunch."

"A what?"

"Intuition. You can sense a connection between this case and our others, but you're uncertain why."

"I'm not enjoying it, the not-knowing-why bit," said Ada. "I should know why."

Mary thought back. "Do you remember, when we

were visiting Newgate Prison, and we weren't sure which hallway to go down?"

Ada nodded. Mary continued.

"You said then that we could pick one, and if we were wrong, the other hallway would still be there. And I must say it made a tremendous amount of sense at the time."

"True," admitted Ada.

"So, if this hunch of yours about the Sons of Bavaria having something to do with the *S* tattoos of our previous cases turns out to be incorrect, you are free to pursue other avenues, as it were."

"Hmm," said Ada, still discontent.

"A hunch is not a bad thing, Ada," assured Mary.

Mary locked the lab's door while Ada went ahead up the stairs, carrying a long brass tube with angled ends.

Ada listened at the door first and, hearing nothing, opened it a crack, poked the brass tube through, and peered into the other end. Inside the tube was a series of lenses and mirrors, and this allowed her to see over tall obstacles or, in this instance, around corners. The coast was clear.

Ada made her way down the deserted corridor

and up the servants' stairs. This led to the upstairs kitchen, and even if she were discovered there, and perhaps scolded for being out of bed, it was familiar enough territory for her.

Yawning, for she was very tired from both that morning's leeching and her very brief adventure downstairs, she looked up and froze.

A pair of painted faces, one man and one woman, peered into the kitchen window from the back garden.

Brandishing her brass periscope, Ada roared and rushed to the window, startling the unusual couple, whose faces quickly bobbed out of sight.

And then Ada did something she had only ever done once before in her eleven-and-almost-twelve-any-day-now years of life.

She fainted.

Ada awoke in her own bed, surrounded by Mary, Anna, Mr. Franklin, and her ostrich of a grandmother. Her first sensation was of something hot and slimy being rubbed against her face, and an odd snarfling and grunting sound in her ear.

"She's awake," said Mary. "Are you all right, Ada?"

Ada looked at the pug, Charlemagne, who had decided all Ada needed was a good snot bath and perhaps some wheezy sniffing. He was quite pleased to see her wake up, because it proved he was correct.

"What happened?" Ada asked, pushing the dog away.

"You fainted, Lady Ada," said Anna.

"Fainted?" Ada asked, indignant. "It's those leeches."

"Regardless," said Gran, "when a young lady faints, she is to aim for the couch. Fainting on the floor is most unbecoming."

"Aim for the . . . good grief," said Ada.

"I've sent for Dr. Polidori," said Gran. "Until he gives you leave, you are to remain in bed, and not get up under any circumstances whatsoever."

"What if there's a fire?" asked Ada.

"Don't be impossible, child," said Gran. "Stay in bed. I shall trust young Mary here to see to it." Her eyebrows sent a very pointed message to Mary, who nodded at them, intimidated.

Lady Noel, Anna, and Mr. Franklin retired from the room, leaving Ada and Mary alone.

"Honestly, Ada, are you sure you're all right?"

"It's just the leeches. Coming up the stairs I got all woozy. And then . . . Oh!"

"Oh?"

"Oh! Painted people in the garden! At the window."

"What are you going on about, Ada?" Mary asked.

"Peeping in the window. A man and a woman, in costume. They looked like dolls, or puppets."

"And are you certain that—"

"That I didn't imagine them? I'm woozy but I'm not bonkers. I ran at them with my periscope, and that's when—"

"You fainted," said Mary calmly.

"Leeches," grumbled Ada.

"Well, do you think these doll people are connected to the Sons of Bavaria?"

"I don't know. We need a plan. We need everybody. And I need a pencil."

"Here," said Mary, handing Ada a pencil and scrap of paper from the bedside.

Ada scribbled. "Send Anna to the chemist, and the tobacconist," she said, and handed the paper to Mary.

"Tobacco snuff, and eucalyptus?" Mary said, reading.

"The sweet stuff in cough medicine. And I'll need one of those *fft fft* things."

"Fft fft?"

"You know, for plants."

"A mister," said Mary.

"Mr. who?" asked Ada.

"I think you're very tired, Ada."

"I think you're right," said Ada sleepily.

Mary smiled and walked quietly out of the room.

REPULSIVE

"Curious," said Dr. Polidori the next morning, in his unplaceable accent. Ada supposed it was, in fact, placeable, as he said it in her bedroom, but she was certain there was more to the word than that.

"What is curious, Doctor?" Ada asked innocently.

"The creatures," he said, meaning the leeches, of course. "They seem . . . disinterested."

"I'm breakfast," Ada answered. "They're always interested."

"Not today," mused the doctor, concerned. "They seem almost repulsed by you."

Ada supposed she ought to have been insulted by the idea of leeches finding her repulsive, but she wasn't.

"Are they all right?" asked Ada, as if out of genuine concern. "Maybe I'm all out of fevered blood? You said they only liked that kind."

"Hmm," hmm'd Polidori, who began collecting the leeches with steel forceps and plopping them back in their glass jar. Clearly vexed, the bushy-eyebrowed doctor did not even say goodbye as he departed, staring into his jar of bloodsucking worms.

He did not notice the brass plant mister on Ada's bedside, nor did he discern the faint scent of distilled tobacco, and eucalyptus.

Alone at last in her room, Ada smiled.

Ada and Mary slipped out of the house through the secret elevator an hour later. Gran hadn't even emerged from her rooms yet this morning, assuming that Ada would still be in bed, being slowly drained.

"Are you sure you're up to this, Ada?" asked Mary.

"Are you mad? I feel fantastic!" Ada answered.

"Full of tigers, once again. Leeches . . ." She made a face. "I showed them."

"You made a secret potion," Mary surmised. "Out of the things Anna brought from the chemist."

"There's a book in the library on India. Loads of leeches there. And they keep them away with a topical tincture of tobacco and eucalyptus. Apparently, leeches hate the taste of the stuff."

"I say, that's terribly clever, if not entirely honest. And you are supposed to be getting better under your doctor's care."

"It was an experiment. Conclusion: Leeches are awful. No more leeches, full of tigers. QED."

Mary did not have enough insight into medicine and leeching to offer an opinion on the matter, but she did respect the extraordinary talents of her friend.

"I dared not call for a carriage," said Mary. "I thought we might find one on the way."

"Oh, we can walk. It's stopped raining. And it's only a mile," said Ada cheerfully. "And I love the smell of the earth after rain. There should be a word for it. Besides, I only have this spoon to carry." Ada held up a rather tarnished old spoon she'd snatched up from the laboratory as they left.

Not knowing what to make of this, Mary changed the subject. "Well, do let me know if you're getting tired. The last time you were out . . ."

"Last time we were out, we were solving a mystery and apprehending clever criminals." They strolled eastward, arm in arm, and occasionally the brims of their bonnets clapped into one another, which made them laugh.

"Not so clever as dastardly, I daresay," noted Mary.

"That's just it," Ada said. "I thought there'd be more solving and less running about."

"Well, it's crime, Ada. It is not as though you are playing chess, and your opponent merely concedes. These are villains. They do villainous things."

"I like the chess-playing part."

"We're still doing quite well in the other part. The chasing-and-catching part. To Allegra's credit," Mary added.

"And Peebs," included Ada.

"And Charles, of course," remembered Mary. "And the constabulary, generally."

"It does seem awfully complicated. It was just going to be the two of us," Ada said as they turned the corner southward. Still a block north of their destination, Ada was delighted to find herself quite untired.

And yet.

The sky was perhaps a shade too blue, and the sun was just a smidge too bright off the white marble. As they approached the construction site of the museum, all the hammering, chipping, snicking, sanding, and dragging was becoming louder and sharper and scratchy in Ada's eyes, in her ears, and on the underside of her skin, until the too-muchness of it all reached Ada's chest, and she found it difficult, suddenly, to remember how to breathe.

"Ada?" Mary sensed something was wrong. Part of this was due to the fact that the younger detective had come to a sudden stop.

"My tongue," Ada said.

"What of it?" Mary asked, concerned.

"Doesn't fit in my mouth properly."

"I'm sure it's fine."

"Not fine. Can't breathe round it," Ada snapped.

"It's . . . you've been inside for quite some time, Ada. Outside is just taking some getting used to."

Ada nodded, so Mary continued.

"And you've done outside loads of times. Long carriage rides all over London."

"Bum-numbing," Ada agreed, trying to catch her breath.

"Exactly. Let's just take your mind off it." Mary looked around for some kind of distraction, anything to redirect Ada from her mounting panic. But everywhere she looked were things belonging to the outside, such as trees, which would just remind Ada that she was not inside, where she'd obviously rather be. Mary looked at Ada herself.

"Spell 'Ada,' " Mary said.

"A-D-A," Ada replied with a quizzical expression.

"How many letters is that?" Mary tried.

"Three," answered Ada. Mary wondered where to go with that and then remembered. "Three's a . . . prime number, isn't it? One of those ones you can't cut in half properly or something."

Ada nodded. "Divisible only by one, and itself."

"But there are others, though, correct?" Mary tried.

"Two, three, five, seven, eleven, thirteen, seventeen, nineteen, twenty-three, twenty-nine, thirty-one, thirty-seven," said Ada, all in a rush.

"And it's also a part of a sequence, isn't it? Three, I mean. When you add a number with the number before it?"

"Fibonacci," Ada said calmly. "Yes: one, one, two, obviously. Then three, five, eight, and five plus eight is thirteen, and thirteen plus eight is twenty-one. It's quite simple."

"I daresay, Ada," said Mary cautiously. "You seem to be breathing quite well."

"Huh," Ada huh'd approvingly. "So I am. Let's press on." And so they did.

In the square in front of the old museum, the new building was taking shape all around them.

"Now, the acquisition is in two days," said Ada. "If I were a clever criminal—"

"Or dastardly," interrupted Mary.

"Or dastardly," agreed Ada, "I would want to keep an eye on things. So we must keep our eyes open for eyers as well as artifacts."

"Right," agreed Mary. "Ready?"

"Ready."

"I'm sorry, ladies, but the museum is closed for a private tour," said the guard.

"Oh, that's all right," said Ada. "We're not here to see the museum." Mary tried to look not too obviously puzzled. She also tried not to look overly sorry for the guard, and whatever was about to happen to him.

"No?" replied the guard. "That's just as well, then."

Ada smiled her most innocent smile, and never stopped smiling in a very pointed fashion.

"Erm," the guard continued. "May I be of some other assistance?"

"Indeed, you may. You may open the door, please," said Ada confidently.

"Ah, you may recall, young lady, our previous conversation in which it was established that the museum is closed."

"Excellent, yes, I do recall," replied Ada.

"So, erm, well," sputtered the guard. "That's a no, then, on the door."

"But we are not here for the museum."

"No?" asked the guard. "Then what are you 'ere for?"

"Well, that's quite a large question, isn't it? Meta-physical, really. I'd love to discuss it with you some-time, perhaps over tea, but right now, we really must be getting on," said Ada.

"What—" began the guard.

"No, 'what' is simply too big a question. Try 'who.'"

"Who?" hazarded the guard.

"And perhaps 'why,'" added Ada.

"Why?" said the guard.

"That's better. We are here to present a valuable historical artifact to the director of acquisitions."

"And what valuable 'istorical artifact might this be, miss?" inquired the guard, unsure if he was sup-posed to be impressed or not, and pretending a little just in case.

Ada presented her spoon with a flourish. "This magnificent specimen was once the Royal Table-spoon of the Court of Eleanor of Aquitaine."

"Ah," said the guard. He paused for a moment. "Ellie who then?"

"Certainly you are familiar with the queen of England from 1154 to 1189? The most adept

stateswoman of the Middle Ages? The mother of Richard the Lion-Heart?"

"Richard the Lion-Heart?" said the guard, now sincerely impressed. "Blimey. And that's his spoon."

"His mother's spoon. She was an extraordinary figure in her own right. You should at least—" Ada was gathering steam.

"That's his spoon, yes," said Mary, her hand on Ada's arm. "And certainly it belongs here, in the British Museum."

"I'm sure it does, miss," agreed the guard.

"Delighted we are indeed to hear it. Now please admit us."

The guard paused. "And do you 'ave an appointment?" he asked.

"But of course we have an appointment," declared Ada. "Miss Newdog here has several, as you can plainly see. Are you not well-appointed, Miss Newdog?" she asked of Mary.

"I do endeavor to be so, Miss Ribbon," said Mary, rejoicing in the use of their clandestine names, reserved exclusively for Wollstonecraft Detective Agency business.

"That's not quite—" began the guard, once again flustered.

"It is, quite. Honestly," assured Ada.

"Quite," agreed Mary.

"Right." The guard nodded. "Well, the director's office is down this hall, to the left all the way at the end. Mind, there's a private tour on, so if you see them, pretend you don't, in a manner of speaking."

Mary was about to thank the poor fellow but saw that Ada had already barreled ahead and was well down the hall, so she scarcely had time for a half nod, half curtsy.

"Richard Lion-Heart's spoon," the guard muttered to himself. "Blimey."

A NUT FOR A JAR
OF TUNA

"I must say, Ada," Mary said, "that was awfully clever. If not frightfully honest."

"I have no way of proving that this spoon did not belong to Eleanor of Aquitaine," said Ada. "That is for the director of acquisitions to decide."

"And are we really going to show it to him?"

"Waste of time. We're here to investigate."

Investigation was clearly going to be a challenge. They were in the older and already-built bit of the museum, and the halls were stacked with crates and bundles waiting to be placed in the new building once it was completed. The halls managed to be both very tidy and a complete mess at the same time, with very few of the exhibits still viewable.

"It all seems rather ordinary," said Mary. "They're getting ready to move, so it's a bit of a jumble."

"Not just ready to move," added Ada, "but expand. A lot of the things in these crates are new. To them, anyway."

"How can you tell?"

"The crates are new. Not all dusty and manky. Some of these things have been in storage for a very long time, but some of them, well, new crates for new things. Or new old things. Old things they just acquired."

"I see," said Mary, who mostly did.

"We may not know until we see it. But I hear that tour coming up behind us."

"Should we hide?" asked Mary.

"We should join," said Ada.

The girls found a gap between two stacks of new crates and wedged themselves in. They heard the tones of an erudite gentleman apologizing for the disarray of the museum generally, and a small party walked past. Silently Ada and Mary filed in at the rear while the tour guide pointed at and spoke about the few visible paintings and artifacts.

Mary found herself quite interested, but Ada's face held a faint scowl. They would follow a procession of large skirts for a half dozen paces, the guide would say something or other for roughly half a minute, and they would all trundle forward another few steps.

"And this unique item, originally designed to adorn an earl, consists of simple trade goods," said the guide.

"Trade goods?" asked a young lady in the small crowd.

"Yes, things that are traded for other things, rather than using coins. A tahiti hat, for example, in exchange for a metal tool. Or simpler," said the guide, "a nut for a jar of tuna."

"What did you say?" asked Ada, pushing forward to see. In a small glass display case was an odd necklace of rough beads—possibly nuts from some exotic tree.

"A nut for a jar of tuna?" Ada repeated.

"Yes, miss . . . umm . . . ," said the puzzled guide, not remembering having seen Ada before, or having her as part of his tour group.

"Who told you to say that?"

"I'm sorry, miss?"

"You said 'a nut for a jar of tuna.' Who told you to say that?"

"Well, it's in the notes we guides are given at the start of each day, when new items arrive."

"And this is a new item?" Ada peered closely at the display. On the glass was a small etched plaque, which read simply ADORN EARL.

"Yes, miss, it arrived only this week, as I recall."

"I'm a fool, aloof am I!" said Ada excitedly.

Mary had no idea what Ada was going on about. Neither did the tour guide.

"Miss?" he said.

"Was it a rat I saw?" said Ada. At this the ladies all looked around nervously.

"No rats, miss! Not at all." He shepherded the tour away quickly. "Now, if I may direct all of your attention to this next item . . . ," the guide continued, with the party following. Ada remained riveted to the spot.

"What are you talking about, Ada?" Mary asked.

"A clue. Two clues, actually. Two clues that lead nowhere, and that get us somewhere."

"If you could possibly back up for a bit and let me catch up . . . ," said Mary.

"Pencil," said Ada, pulling out a folded yellow sheet of paper. She pulled off her right glove with her teeth, biting the tip of one of her fingers. Mary obliged after digging through her own purse. Ada wrote a short sentence and handed this to Mary.

"A nut for a jar of tuna?" asked Mary, reading.

"Now read it backward," said Ada.

"A nut for . . . I say, that's rather clever, isn't it? But what does it mean?"

"Nothing! It's just a palindrome, a word or phrase that's the same backward as forward. Like 'tahiti hat' or 'bird rib' or 'don't nod' or 'evil olive.' Now try this." Ada took back the paper and wrote two words.

"Adorn Earl? I'm trying to read it backward, but it doesn't make any sense."

"Because that one isn't backward. It's an anagram. Remember, Miss Anning was sent to a location in Dorset. . . ."

"Yes, and she said she couldn't find it," said Mary.

"Precisely. Doesn't exist. Because it's not a place; it's a puzzle. Look," said Ada, taking back the paper yet again and scribbling more before handing it to Mary.

ADORN EARL

LEARN ROAD

"Honestly, Ada, I'm trying but I still . . . ," Mary began.

Ada took the paper back once more, wrote again, and returned the paper so that it now read:

ADORN EARL

LEARN ROAD

NORA RADEL

"Good heavens," said Mary. "But what does it mean?"

"It simply means," said Ada, "that she is trying to get our attention. She's waving 'hello' at us."

"So . . ." Mary hesitated. "What should we do now?"

"We should wave back."

Ada marched on, clearly excited, while Mary trailed in her wake. Mary fully expected Ada to retrace their course through the museum, and wondered what story would be presented to the unfortunate and befuddled security guard. Yet just as she prepared to follow Ada to the right, Ada darted left, through a great doorway, and entered a long, white, and soaring gallery. It had two stories, as it was ringed by a railed balcony glossed with lead-white paint. On the floor were crates and cases bigger than Ada's bleh, and Mary watched her friend weave between them on some mission she herself could not discern.

"Ada," Mary whispered as loud as she dared, "where are we going?"

"Scene of the crime," said Ada, without regard for the volume of her voice.

"The dognapping? That was in Lyme Regis."

"Not that crime," said Ada. "The next one."

The girls had seemed to reach their destination. Beautiful arching double doors in stout oak— one slightly ajar. Through it Mary could glimpse a courtroom—or at least a room as she had always imagined one to look like. A red carpet, paneled walls, and a judge's bench with a gavel.

Ada slipped inside, with Mary fast behind her.

It was not a courtroom, she realized, but it was close enough. Instead of benches for witnesses arranged around the great room, there were tables for exhibits, each one draped and labeled. The one closest to her was marked 284A, which she did not find to be terribly illuminating.

"This must be the auction room," Mary guessed. To the right of the door the girls had entered through stood a main exit, or entrance, she supposed, with no fewer than five sets of double doors for the admission of the public. Through the glass of the doors, Mary could make out a cobbled courtyard, and a green beyond.

"Yes," Ada confirmed. "Not sure why they call it an auction, but this is where they acquire things. Buy things, once someone clever and important, like Miss Anning, says the things are real. This makes it official."

Before each hidden exhibit was a small wooden easel, with brass hinges.

"What are these for?" Mary inquired.

"Documents," Ada replied. "The statements by the clever and important people. That say the things are what they are supposed to be." Ada didn't look at Mary through all of this, nor did the inflection of her voice change. She was looking for something, counting down, which took up the parts of her brain other people use for chatting and explaining things. "Aha," she said finally. "Two twenty-one B."

The box, for indeed it was a box, was barely a forearm deep, though it was twice as long as Mary's arms spread wide. Without any concern for clandestineness, Ada tugged on the canvas drape, and the box wobbled threateningly.

Ada stared at the revelation for a full second.

"Fake," she said, and tried to fling the canvas back over the box. Mary had hardly any time to inspect it, only catching a glimpse of an animal skeleton in white plaster.

"You seem very sure," said Mary, smoothing out the canvas. As she was taller than her friend, Mary was able to set the cloth to rights again.

Ada stood stock-still for a second, gestured with an open hand in Mary's direction, and added a single word.

"Paper."

BROBDINGNAGIAN

A few minutes later, the girls were back in the bustling main courtyard, where they dodged masons'
carts and cranes and workmen.

A large basket swung toward them, accompanied
by a shout of "Watch out!"

Ada and Mary ducked as the enormous wicker
cube, creaking on giant ropes, nearly knocked their
bonnets off. The package landed heavily on the gravel
in front of them.

"What is it?" Ada asked a workman as he jumped
from his crane to be sure they were all right.

"Cotton, miss, from America. For packing up the displays, afore we move 'em," he said.

"No, no. What's this basket?"

"It's just a cotton crate, miss. Bit larger than we usually see 'em. Like a giant's picnic basket, eh? Brobdingnagian."

Mary was impressed by the word.

Ada was impressed by the basket. . . .

They began to walk north, and the hammering began to grow distant. Ada was elated, despite not having found anything that seemed directly pertinent to the case.

"Oh, oh, I can see why she likes this," said Ada, grinning.

"Who?" asked Mary.

"Nora Radel! Once she finds the note we left her, it should all get rather more interesting between me and my archnemesis."

"Archnemesis? Nora Radel is your enemy?" Mary asked. Then, "Wait—I thought you left that note on the display for the Sons of Bavaria? What did you say?"

"Yes, yes. They are in this together. My note simply says that the Sons of Bavaria have the wrong dog. And that we have the right dog, Miss Anning's dog. Also that we are perfectly happy for them to go through with their plan of forcing her to authenticate the fake ichthyosaur so long as we get half the money."

"I say . . . isn't that . . . criminal?" said Mary.

"It's not a real plan," said Ada. "It's a counterfeit plan, because we are counterfeit criminals, and those are counterfeit dinosaur bones. That is why this will work. I've signed it with a counterfeit criminal name."

"You have a counterfeit criminal name?"

"The Sphinx of Black Quartz," said Ada decisively. "Only it's not my criminal name. It's hers. Or at least it's one of my current theories."

"You've lost me completely," said Mary.

"The Sons of Bavaria won't understand. They'll panic, and they'll be afraid. But she'll know. And that's what matters."

Mary and Ada walked past Marylebone Road and found the gate to the servants' alley, which ran behind the row of great houses. They opened the gate discreetly and crunched their way along the gravel to Ada's back garden. By using servants' paths and the back door, they hoped to avoid Lady Noel.

But as they approached the back door to the upstairs kitchen, the door opened of its own accord. Or, rather, according to a white-gloved and bewigged footman of Gran's. Gran herself stood stock-still just inside the doorway, expressionless.

"Good afternoon, Lady Noel," Mary began. "We were just in the garden, taking some air." She felt bad for lying, but it clearly wasn't working, and she wasn't sure if that should make her feel better or worse.

"Miss Godwin," said Gran, her snarfling pug clutched to her chest, "you have proven your company to be a detriment to Lady Ada's recovery. Therefore, your services are no longer required."

"Services?" said Ada. "Mary is my friend!"

"And see how excitable such a friendship has made you!" chided Gran. "To bed with you at once, child, and I shall fetch the doctor to see what harm this 'air' you speak of has inflicted. As for you, Miss Godwin, it is inappropriate that you should enter this house."

"Inappropriate?" said Mary, offended.

"Don't talk back, child; it is unbecoming for a young lady. Ada, bed, now. Good day, Miss Godwin."

"But—" Mary began.

"Good. Day," pronounced Gran as she took a hand from Charlemagne and grabbed Ada's arm roughly, pulling her inside.

The footman closed the door, not with a slam but with an emphatic click that was at once perfectly appropriate and utterly dismissive.

Mary stood alone in the garden as the December rain resumed.

Anna had also clearly been given a stern talking-to from Gran, for she said little as she helped Ada out of her clothes and into her nightdress, tucking her back into bed.

Ada surprised herself a little. She should be furious, fuming, outraged.

Incendiary.

Instead, she felt unperturbed, and said so.

"I am unperturbed. This changes nothing." Ada

wondered briefly if there was such a word as "perturbed" and realized there must be, and she made a mental note to look it up after.

"It would seem, Lady Ada, that with everyone banished from the house, and you confined to bed, it must change everything."

"It's still a good plan," mused Ada.

"Lady Ada," Anna said, "your grandmother has her footmen stationed at every entrance to the house, with strict orders that you are not to leave under any circumstances."

"That's not fair," said Ada. "She can't send me to bed. I'm a criminal mastermind." She paused for a moment and added, "More or less."

"That's as may be, Lady Ada," said Anna. "However."

"Still a good plan," repeated Ada, with a grumble this time.

Ada pondered while Anna brushed and put away Ada's clothes.

"Can you send some letters for me?" Ada asked.

"I can certainly try, Lady Ada," answered Anna. "But I fear that Lady Noel is watching me very carefully. Any letter I send for you is likely to be read. She doesn't want you excited."

"Hmm," said Ada. "One that I have in mind is pretty exciting. We'll have to be clandestine." Ada had a thought. "Can Mrs. . . . Chowser do it?" she said, thinking of the cook.

Anna smiled. "You remembered her name! Well-done. Yes, I'm sure she will run a special errand for you and deliver your letter."

"It's a good plan," said Ada once again, a little more at ease. And she settled in to make more good plans involving seamstresses, ship riggers, and a quantity of coal. . . .

INGREDIENTS

Ada awoke before the dreary dawn. And she felt marvelous. Electric. It was as though she had spent several weeks being sucked dry by leeches, only to then spend an entire day not being sucked dry by leeches.

It was too soon to expect a reply from Miss Anning—Mrs. Chowser had delivered the note detailing Ada's plan to the Golden Alder Inn only the previous evening. But there was much to prepare to put her plans into action. She needed supplies.

Under Ada's bed were a pair of slippers and a cast-iron pot. At the pot's bottom was some kind of charred material, which she couldn't quite remember putting in there or setting on fire, not exactly, and thought she should best chip it out before anything else went in there, just in case. This she did with the aid of a very large wrench, which while barely fitting in the pot did an excellent job of crushing the black gunk into soot, which Ada poured into the fireplace grate. Mostly.

The potassium nitrate crystals, which she had saved from a previous experiment involving a cannon, were precisely where she had left them. The rest were baking supplies, and that meant the kitchen.

Ada opened her door silently and looked for her grandmother's watchful footmen. Seeing none, she nearly went down the main stairway out of habit, but then chose the servants' stairs, just in case. The dawn offered just enough light to let her go about without a candle, which would have drawn attention.

The first stair gave a terrible creak that Ada knew was louder in her head than it was in the house. Still, she held her breath as she crept her way down to the upstairs kitchen, and down further to the servants' hall, and the main kitchen in the back. There was a flicker of firelight, the coals still glowing from the night before. Ada's shadow stretched long and strange against the bricks of the kitchen wall.

She had brought nothing with her, but found a cup for the brown sugar and baking soda she needed. The scrape of the heavy sugar jar against the counter was ominous, as was the tick of the spoon against the cup, each sound a little threat, plotting to give her away.

What would she say if she were caught? Baking muffins? Ada had no recipe for muffins, and had never made any and had no idea how, so any lie would be unconvincing. Ada of course knew the recipe for many other things, but none of them were edible and most were at least slightly dangerous.

Her pilfered cup full to the brim with what she needed, she retraced her steps up all the way to the hall outside her own bedroom door, wincing at each squeak and groan of the house. She closed her door with a regrettably loud click, but no one seemed to hear.

Now there was the simple matter of fire. Coals and kindling and matches in the firebox beside the fireplace in her bedroom. She had seen Anna do this a thousand times, or at least been in the room while she did it, though it proved more difficult than Ada expected. There was too much smoke, until she realized the flue was closed and sorted out which way the stubby iron lever went to open the chimney.

She placed all the ingredients in the pot—sugar, baking soda, and potassium nitrate—giving them a stir with the enormous wrench before placing the whole works on the glowing coals.

Ada heard the sounds of the house waking up— the waking up was louder now that the house was full of a more appropriate number of servants. When it had been just one butler, one maid, one cook, and one governess, the amount of noise was barely a distraction. But now the house felt more like a ship at sea, with constant scurrying and opening and closing and unfurling and shuffling. She kept an eye on the pot—the trick was to melt the ingredients together, but not actually cook them, and Ada grew increasingly uncertain as to what the difference was, exactly.

She used a wadded-up shawl as a pot holder and pulled the concoction off the coals to rest on the tiles in front of the fireplace. It gave off a smell that was both sweet and salty at the same time. Perfect.

Now it was simply a matter of letting the goo cool before—

The door opened.

Ada jumped at the surprise, though not as much as Anna, who had brought more coals for the fire, expecting Ada to be asleep.

"Experiment," whispered Ada. "Shut the door."

"Whatever are you making, Lady Ada?" Anna whispered back.

"Muffins?" tried Ada.

Anna looked unconvinced at the pot of brown sludge, with the wrench sticking out of it, so large it nearly toppled the whole thing over.

"Well, as long as it's not some sort of bomb," said Anna nervously.

Ada looked immediately guilty.

"Ah," Anna said.

SHILLINGS

11

Charles had been well pleased to receive a note from Lady Ada, requesting his help with some clandestine observations.

Sleuth-hounding was how he liked to think of it: a trail dog sniffing to see if the hunter is headed in the right direction. The note had come with two silver shillings—certainly more than a day's wages, although he'd have to give one to the foreman in exchange for the day off work.

He was shooed out of his morning carriage by a

pair of spinsters horrified to find him reading inside, so he had walked the mile to the boot-polish factory and its wax-and-sulfur smell that he never entirely got out of his hair or clothes.

A little girl tried to sell him an apple, and he took in how tired she looked, like she'd been up all night. Unfortunately, he hadn't the pennies to spare, and the shilling was too great a thing to part with. He did smile at her, but when he reached out to pat her head, she bolted backward as though she expected to be struck. This saddened him, and he continued walking, having to step across a sleeping pair of scruffy-looking men on the way.

"Allo allo allo, wot's this, then?" asked his foreman, sleeves rolled up past his large, pointy elbows, and dark eyes leering out from under the brim of his cap. "Guttersnipe's late for work this mornin'."

"Actually, sir, I believe I'm a few minutes earl—"

"Oh, 'sir' izzit? Don't you sir me, boy; I work for a livin'. Now you get your laggard behind inna that there line, boy, or I'll give you what for and no gullin'."

"Actually," said Charles, presenting the shilling, "I was hoping we could again make our arrangement."

The foreman plucked the silver coin from Charles's hand.

"Arrangement, now? We've no arrangement, boy, 'side from me not boxin' your ears 'ere at the present moment for your guff! You're touched in the 'ead if you reckon you'll be spendin' the day like some gentleman wiv 'is feet up!'"

"But I have paid you a shilling, which is more than enough to—"

"I say it's my shilling, right and proper, for teachin' you a lesson about puttin' on airs, my son, my son! Take a lot more than one shilling for me to be turnin' a blind eye to your slothful ways."

Charles steeled himself and locked eyes with the cantankerous foreman. "Two shillings."

"'Ow'd you get two shillings, then?"

"Never you mind. Two shillings, and I will be off for the day."

"Let's see it, this shilling of yours."

"You'll find it looks like the one I just gave you," Charles replied.

"Oh! 'oo sets a flash o' merriment wont to set the table on a roar, eh? Don't you get clever wiv me, lad."

"Two shillings, in total," said Charles, handing over the prized second coin.

"'At's more like it, that is. Now off wiv ya."

"Thank you, and I shall see you tomorrow," said Charles with as much courtesy as he could manage.

"Oh, I fink not, my boy. Reliable employment is wot I offer, not this comes-as-'e-pleases. We's partin' ways, you 'n me, we is."

Charles's stomach tightened. He needed this job, and desperately. Not only to pay his board with Mrs. Roylance, stingy as she was with soup and coal, but also to help his father in debtor's prison. At fourteen, Charles knew his earnings were all that stood between his family and further ruin.

"But surely two shillings . . ." He couldn't believe what had just happened.

"Cost of an education, that is. Now be off wiv you, 'fore I 'ave to knock out your 'ampsteads."

Still in shock, and lamenting the two shillings lost but not seeing any way of retrieving them, Charles turned away from his former employer. Retracing his steps up the cobbled block, he again crossed the sleeping men, and passed the filthy little girl, still offering her one polished apple. His stomach growled, and the sound alone was enough to send her scurrying this time.

HERALDRY

Ada stowed the now-cooled pot back under her bed and fell into a book, and then another. Eventually, Gran appeared to check in on her, and Charlemagne nearly discovered the pot, the contents of which by this time had set into a stiff brown glue. Mercifully, Dr. Polidori had been called away and was not able to attend to Ada today. Gran withdrew, scooping up her pug and reminding Ada that she was not to get out of bed under any circumstance whatsoever.

Whatsoever, thought Ada, checking the clock. *We'll see about that.*

Anna entered not long after with a tray for breakfast and the *Times*. Ada scanned the tray for envelopes and saw none.

"I was hoping for a reply from Miss Anning," Ada said irritably.

"There's that, and more," said Anna with a grin. She placed the tray down at the foot of Ada's bed and turned to the door. Glancing both ways down the hall, she made a beckoning motion, and in walked . . .

Anna. Another Anna. Wearing an identical black dress with an identical white apron and an identical white mobcap. Only, beneath the cap were wisps of hair the color of which Ada would recognize anywhere. Oh, and there was the face too, Ada realized.

"Mary?"

Mary curtsied and smiled broadly in her maid's outfit as Anna closed the door.

"I thought this would surprise you," said Anna.

"Extraordinary," said Ada. "How did you get past . . ."

"Oh, the house is positively crawling with servants," said Anna, "and Lady Noel is hiring more by the day. A new face wouldn't catch notice even if we had the time to look, which we don't."

"And," said Mary, "we have this." She pulled an envelope out from her apron. "A letter from Miss Anning."

Ada was impatient to read it but tried not to snatch it from Mary's hand. Anna smiled and withdrew as Mary handed it over.

The paper was a pale green and, once the seal was broken, was revealed to be stationery from the inn where Miss Anning was staying in London. At the top of the page was a heraldic shield, like a medieval knight's, and upon it an alder tree in gold. The letter read:

> Dear Lady Byron,
>
> I must thank you again for your kind offer of assistance.
>
> You have tried your best; however, I am afraid I find your plans as outlined insufficient—in fact, you may have made things worse, and I am unwilling to cooperate. If you succeed in convincing the Sons of Bavaria they have the wrong dog, how will the right dog ever be restored to me? You may thwart the

counterfeiters, and save my reputation,
but I care not for either if I lose my dog.

I now understand why you are re-
ferred to as the second cleverest girl in
England.

Very sincerely yours,
M. Anning

Ada was flabbergasted. How could Miss Anning, clearly a brilliant mind, not see the genius in Ada's plan? And who was it who had told Miss Anning that Ada was the second cleverest girl in England? And there was something fishy about the stationery, and perhaps the handwriting, but Ada was too upset to take it in fully.

"Oh, Ada," said Mary, "I'm so sorry."

"It's a good plan. This makes no sense," Ada insisted.

"Well, she is no doubt worried half to death over her poor dog; she may not be making the best of decisions."

"It's the worst of decisions!" protested Ada. "I have a plan. A good one!"

"What was your plan for getting out of here?"

Mary said, hoping to distract Ada. "Your grand-mother has servants all the way between the hall and the laboratory, so there's no getting out that way."

"Oh, that. I made a bomb," said Ada.

"A what?" Mary gasped.

"Not a bomb bomb, just a smoke bomb. So they'd think the house was on fire, and everybody would run out, and I could stop the acquisition."

"Well," said Mary, "I was thinking you could just borrow another maid's costume from Anna and sneak out the servants' entrance."

Ada paused. "Your plan is better."

Anna returned with a bundle in brown paper, and within it was a dress and apron for Ada.

Mary and Anna helped Ada into it, and they could see at once that everything was entirely too big. Ada looked in the glass.

"I look like a mouse in a dog suit," said Ada.

"I can fix that," Anna said, and fussed around Ada with pins. The result was a bit of a mess. "Well, it will have to do long enough to get you out," Anna said.

"I could still pretend the house is on fire," said Ada.

"Let's not resort to that quite yet, shall we?" Mary suggested.

"Right, here we go," said Anna. "The coast is clear."

Anna, Ada, and Mary left the bedroom and were about to descend the servants' stairs when a near parade of footmen came up them. Anna sharply turned her back and descended the main staircase, so Ada and Mary followed suit, with Ada lifting the hem of her dress lest she trip and tumble.

The front door was so close.

A murmur of footmen came from the parlor, some business among them briefly distracting them from the grand front door of the Marylebone house, the guardianship of which had fallen to one lone individual. One enormously tall, solid, and ever-silent individual.

Mr. Franklin.

Anna curtsied, eyes downcast, and spun away from the group back to her duties. Mary and Ada didn't even try to fool Mr. Franklin. Ada merely looked up at him with pleading eyes, and he opened the door, using his own large frame to block any sight of the departing girls. The door closed, he tugged at the front of his jacket and pulled up his gloves.

ADJACENCIES

Once outside, the girls continued the charade of errand-maids, with Ada's hands clutching her over-long dress. She'd never before in her life given a thought to getting dirty, but these weren't her clothes, and she was doing her best to weave between the muddier of the puddles and the freshest plops of horse poo.

The girls crossed the road and rounded the corner, and they were free from the row of perfect white houses surrounded moatlike by the grey filth of the street.

"Plan?" whispered Mary.

"Book," answered Ada, producing a small volume from behind her apron. *"The Abraham Hanover Guide to the Fraternal Orders, Clubs, and Societies of London,* published in 1818."

"Would a society from Lyme Regis in Dorset be in there?"

"Any society from anywhere is also in London. Says so in chapter one," Ada answered.

"And the Sons of Bavaria are in there?"

"They are not. Which means either that they are newer than when this book came out or that they are made-up."

"Is Bavaria new?" Mary asked.

"No, no. It's allied with Germany. Very old. So if there were a Fraternal Order, Club, or Society of their Sons, you'd think it would be in place before the publication of this book."

"So, what do we look for?"

"Commonalities. Similarities. Adjacencies. Just like in number sets."

"I don't follow, Ada dear," admitted Mary.

"There's a Sons of Bolivia. Also a Sons of Belgravia—we'll go there first—and a Sons of Bohemia."

"Adjacencies, things next to each other," said Mary, getting it now, at least a little.

There was a map in Ada's book. All the locations had been circled by Ada in pencil, and they all lay to the south, and at least a little to the east.

"These . . . these aren't the safest places in the world," said Mary. "Not for two young girls. We should have brought Mr. Franklin." Then Mary laughed at the thought.

"Is that funny?" Ada asked.

"Well, it's not terribly . . . clandestine," said Mary. "As kindly as we know him to be, he's something of a monster."

"Is he?" asked Ada, who genuinely hadn't noticed.

"Ada, he's eight feet tall. And he never says a word! His main skill seems to be looming and casting oppressive shadows. If one were not familiar with how . . . how extraordinarily trustworthy he is, one would be rather intimidated indeed. I imagine that's why your mother left you with him."

"Why?" Ada wondered.

"To keep you safe," Mary said. "I don't know if he even has a first name. He seems to have sprouted fully formed from the marble as some kind of sentry."

"Adam," Ada said. "His first name is Adam."

"Well-done, Ada. How do you know that?"

"I'm . . . I'm not sure," she said quietly. She paused for a moment as the bells in the parish church tolled the hour. "We should get a carriage," Ada said. "Charles will be waiting."

The rain had quickened, and there seemed little point in exiting the carriage. The first hall was squeezed between rather seedy-looking establishments; and beneath the hastily painted sign, SONS OF BELGRAVIA, and a sloppy cartoon of a coat of arms was a CLOSDE sign on the doorknob.

A figure, instantly recognizable as Charles, approached, and it seemed to Mary that he was trying his very best to appear cheerful. Charles entered the carriage, courtesies were exchanged, and the trio got on with the business of sleuthing.

"What goes on in there?" asked Mary.

"Gentlemen from similar walks of life join these sorts of things for 'fraternity, kinship, and support,' as they say," answered Charles. "Mostly, this seems to

involve playing cards and singing songs from wherever they're from, and loaning money to the widows
after the members die."

"That hardly sounds sinister," said Mary.

"It isn't. Which either makes it the worst place
to find criminals, or the best place to hide them,"
Charles said.

"It's taxonomy, really," Ada interjected.

Mary recalled the lessons of the other morning.
"Kingdom, phylum, and whatnot?"

"Yes," said Ada. "Big groupings, then littler
groupings, until you find the species. In this case,

fraternal organizations, fraternal organizations of London, fraternal organizations of London beginning with *B* and ending with *A,* fraternal organizations of London beginning with *B* and ending with *A* who kidnap people's dogs and sell counterfeit ichthyosaur bones."

"But what if it doesn't follow? What if the dognappers and counterfeiters aren't actually a fraternal organization of London beginning with *B* and ending with *A* at all?" asked Mary.

"Then we have them in the wrong taxonomy, and have to start over. Still, on to the next one." Ada knocked on the roof of her carriage, and it lurched to the next location through a dense silver forest of rain.

The Sons of Bolivia presented a similar spectacle— a closed hall between two shops, both seeming down on their luck. The Bolivians had a slightly newer flag, in red, gold, and green. Clearly, such places were hired because the rent was cheap, and the Sons of such fraternities were of modest means. The carriage lurched to the Sons of Bohemia hall, and while this one looked older, it was likewise an innocent place of gathering for tired men enduring hard life, finding friendship among their compatriots.

"So, nothing, then," said Mary in defeat.

"Absolutely nothing," Ada agreed.

"I'm terribly sorry I have failed to be more useful," said Charles.

"Waste of time, I fear," sighed Mary.

"Not at all!" exclaimed Ada. "This is science. Finding nothing out of the ordinary is just as important as finding a sign saying CRIMINAL HIDEOUT. It gives us a point of information."

"Like your bleh spindles," said Mary.

"Just like that. There's a hole in the stick, and either I put a peg in it or I don't. In this case, here are three holes, one for each of the Sons of Whomever, and not one of them gets a peg."

"That's still nothing, Lady Ada," said Charles.

"That's a pattern, Charles. A pattern is never nothing."

"So what does it tell us, then?" Mary was frustrated, and didn't understand why her friend was not.

"It tells us that there is no such thing as the Sons of Bavaria. Our dognappers are using a counterfeit name."

"Why would grocers need a counterfeit name?"

"Because they want to be clandestine. And because the Dognapping Grocers—assuming they are, in fact, grocers—is hardly an intimidating name. Just like Mr. Franklin. He may be harmless but he doesn't seem so."

"So the Sons of Bavaria are using an assumed name to appear to be more . . . organized? Wicked?" Charles asked.

"Well, it's better than the Sons of Bacteria," Ada said. And then she laughed and laughed to herself. Mary, not getting the joke, but eventually finding Ada's laughter contagious, joined in. The carriage rocked with giggling all the way home to Marylebone Road.

"I'm glad you're pleased, Lady Ada," Charles said as they descended from the carriage and took refuge from the rain beneath a tree. "But I must confess I'm at something of a loss here. Perhaps you see something which I myself am unable to."

"Right," said Ada. "Let's say you find a dog. You're not a clever criminal, you're just awful, all right? And instead of wanting to give the dog back, you want to get something in exchange for the dog."

"Wouldn't most people offer a reward for the dog's return?" suggested Mary.

"Would they?" asked Ada.

"Usually one might offer, yes. Although it would be improper to accept."

"Ah yes, but they're awful, remember?" Ada continued, drawing out her theory. "So you wouldn't care if it was improper to accept. In fact, you'd want more than what was usually offered. Hang on, is the offer a lot?"

"Not usually, no," said Charles. "A token, really."

"There you go," said Ada. "You're awful, and you want a lot. So you do a little digging, and you find you've got the dog of a world-famous scientist, someone whom the British Museum relies upon to authenticate fossils. And these fossils fetch a lot of money. . . ." Ada trailed off, and returned. "Do they?"

"Do they what, Ada?" Mary asked.

"Fetch a lot of money?"

"I can only assume so, yes," answered Mary. "A great deal."

"There you are. Scads of money. But the thing is, you're not very clever, or very criminal. You need help. So you ask. This . . . ," Ada struggled, "is the big equation. We've been looking at the small equation; a dognapping, extortion—the bit with the counterfeit dinosaur bones. Easiest case ever. We know who did what and how and why. No, the real equation to solve, the big one, is that not-so-clever criminals are getting help to pull off clever crimes, pretending to be all manner of things for no other reason, it seems, than to get my attention. And it's working."

"Whom would one ask for help in being criminal?" Charles asked.

"The so-called cleverest girl in England, I suspect," Ada answered.

"Nora Radel," Mary said, finally understanding.

"It's just a . . . a hunch," Ada said, accepting both word and circumstance. "But let's say not-so-clever criminals know they can call on Nora Radel, and she will tell them what to do. She devises a criminal name for them, a story, about being a fraternal organization, although I don't understand that bit just yet. She finds the counterfeit fossil, or has it made, and puts all the variables together. And now the not-so-clever criminals have a relatively clever crime."

"A consulting criminal," mused Mary. It seemed terrifying and brilliant all at once, which she supposed was the point.

Charles nodded, but there was a shadow across his face that seemed to Mary to be unrelated to the case. She tried to inquire quietly, but he shook his head and said he must be off in search of new employment. He tipped his cap and hurried away.

"Charles has lost his employment, it seems," said Mary as she and Ada approached the house.

"What?" asked Ada.

"His job. He doesn't have one anymore. Because of us, I suspect. Or, rather, because of his always taking time away to help us."

"What was his job?"

"I seem to recall he worked at the boot-polish factory. Gluing the labels on."

"That sounds . . . um . . ."

"It is, or was, rather," said Mary.

"Well, he won't miss that much."

"It's not the job, Ada. It's the money. Ordinary people have to work, to make money, to support their families."

"I hadn't thought of that," admitted Ada, and felt bad that she hadn't.

"Well," assured Mary, giving Ada's arm a squeeze. "We shall have to come up with something for him. Perhaps Peebs can help."

Ada nodded. She was unused to the idea of Peebs being helpful, but he'd proven himself to be so on at least two occasions. Perhaps he could make it three.

DOGNAPPING

As the girls had hoped, Mr. Franklin awaited their arrival on the steps to the house. In a gesture that under other circumstances would have appeared rude, he opened the door, looked up and down the various corridors that led to the entrance, and then turned back to them and nodded.

They slipped into the house, having forgotten, for a moment, that they were in disguise, until Anna arrived from the kitchen and goggled at them. All three looked at one another comically.

A bark rang out, and the trio turned at once to

the source of the sound—Charlemagne, in the parlor. There, inside the house, stood two people, a man and a woman, painted like dolls, clearly attempting to kidnap the pug.

All involved were trying not to draw attention to themselves, with the exception, of course, of the dog. Anna, Ada, and Mary froze, within bolting distance of the front door, and likewise the would-be dognappers stood stock-still.

"Tick," said the unusually painted woman.

"Tock," said the man, with the same white powder and round red circles on his cheeks.

It struck Ada as a curious thing to say. However, the only thing it occurred to Ada to say in reply was "AAAAAAAH!" at the top of her lungs, while charging toward the couple.

The doll people panicked and threw the small dog at the trio of maids. Ada stepped on her too-long dress and fell to the floor, but Mary caught Charlemagne in midair. The pair of puppets pushed Anna into Mr. Franklin, opened the front door, and were on their way before Ada found her feet.

There was a further commotion outside as the fleeing duo ran straight into and knocked over an

arriving Peebs, who was hurled into a hedgerow. Mr. Franklin set Anna to rights, then immediately dispatched himself to render assistance to Peebs.

"Good heavens," said Mary. "What was that all about?"

"Dognapping," said Ada. "Attempted. She got my message."

"Who got what message?" asked Anna, quite disturbed.

"Sons of Bavaria," Ada explained. "By way of my archnemesis. They think we have the real Tray. Miss Anning's dog. It means the plan is working."

"But who were those tick-tock people?" Mary asked. "They're not the Sons of Bavaria that Miss Anning described, bearded men with their sleeves rolled up and no discernible accent."

"No, but I've seen them before, out the window," Ada said. "Eyeing up the place. They're part of her plan; I'm sure of it."

"Part of whose plan?" asked an imperious voice.

Gran stood disapprovingly, flanked by two footmen.

"Certainly not, I hope, a plan to impersonate my servants and insinuate yourself in this house, Miss

Godwin," Gran continued. "And certainly not a plan to extricate yourself from your bed rest, Ada. And you, Miss . . ."

"Anna, ma'am," said Anna.

"I should dismiss you from service altogether, were we not so miserably shorthanded here. But I trust this is the last you shall aid and abet Lady Ada in her excitability."

"Yes, ma'am," said Anna, who curtsied and shuffled out of the room.

Peebs arrived, followed by a silent Mr. Franklin, still brushing boxwood from his coat.

"Here is your dog," said Mary, handing Charlemagne over to Lady Noel. "We rescued him."

"From whom?" Gran demanded.

"Intruders, Lady Noel. Bent on the abduction of your beloved animal."

"Nonsense," insisted Gran. "I've had a footman stationed at every entrance in the event of an escape attempt. The only intruder, Miss Godwin, is yourself. My servants shall show you out."

"Actually, Lady Noel, if I may—" Peebs began.

"You may not" was Gran's decisive reply.

Mary was on the verge of tears, her plans

overthrown and herself being barred from her friend's house twice in as many days.

Ada reached out and gave Mary's hand a squeeze.

As she walked past Peebs, Mary dared not meet his eyes lest she burst into tears.

"Don't give up," whispered Peebs.

BAVARIA

15

Moments later, Ada was yet again in her nightdress, and Anna sat on a chair, removing the pins from her uniform.

Peebs knocked on the door and was admitted. Upon seeing Anna, he gave her a courteous nod, which she returned.

"It seems," he said to Ada, "that your grandmother has decided that my tutelage is not too exciting for you, so that is precisely what you are to be subjected to."

"What?" asked Ada crossly.

"I'm boring, so I am to be your punishment."

"Makes sense," Ada agreed.

"Steady on," said Peebs, slightly insulted.

"No, she's just like that," said a resigned Ada. "Where's Mary?"

"Mr. Franklin was directed to escort her home, personally."

"Oh," said Ada sadly. "How are you here?"

"How, Lady Ada?"

"Banished. All my father's friends. And my mother wrote that you were to be banished, specifically."

"Ah, well," Peebs chuckled. "Lady Noel neglected to ask my name. She has thus far referred to me as 'Mr. Peebs' and has not as yet discerned my actual identity, nor would this seem to be a priority. Too boring even for her, it appears." He smiled.

"Miss Anna," continued Peebs, "was this your doing, the scheme to introduce Miss Godwin into the house by way of subterfuge?"

"I'm sorry, Mr. Shelley," said Anna. "Subterfuge?"

"Sneakiness," said Ada.

"Ah," answered Anna, "I'm afraid, sir, the answer is yes."

"Well-done, then," said Peebs with a smile. Anna blushed a little.

"Enough!" said Ada. "We've got to stop the acquisition at the museum, and it's tomorrow! With or without Miss Anning's approval."

"Why?" asked Peebs. Ada made a face. "No, please don't misunderstand me. I know why. And I applaud your sense of justice in the matter. Science itself is the prey here. But insofar as Miss Anning is concerned, are her interests not served by her playing along and seeing the return of her dog?"

"I'm . . . she was . . ." Ada was frustrated. She knew what Peebs was asking, but she was too angry to find the words. Not angry at Peebs, but at Gran for placing her under house arrest. Angry at Miss Anning for not believing in her. Angry at herself for not being clever enough to find a way around this situation.

"She was," Peebs began, "a girl, like you. A girl of science, who has become a woman of science, and made a remarkable contribution, as you hope to. And her reputation is that of your future, and it is this you seek to defend."

"Oh!" said Anna, impressed at this insight. Ada merely harrumphed.

"Sons of Bavaria," Ada said. "What do you know?"

"Well, Miss Mary has briefed me that they are the alleged organization behind Miss Anning's dognapping. However . . ."

"Yes?" asked Ada.

"Well, there appears to be some sort of jest involved, a reference to the Bavarian Illuminati. I mean, if one is to pretend to have a vast conspiracy behind oneself, one can hardly choose a more suitable pedigree."

"Explain."

"Well, the Bavarian Illuminati were a very real gathering of intellectuals that began in 1776. They opposed what they felt were corrupting influences on government, and their ideals influenced the French Revolution. Although the society itself was outlawed and officially disbanded before that—the government not liking their tone at all—many pretenders since have claimed to be among their members, or to be from a secretly surviving part of the society itself."

"But?"

"Such claims are undoubtedly spurious," Peebs concluded.

"Spurious?" asked Anna. "Oh," she said, realizing she properly ought not to be listening. "Pardon me."

"Spurious," said Ada. "Counterfeit. As fake as those ichthyosaur bones."

"Indeed, Lady Ada," said Peebs. "I suspect someone is having you on."

"Fishy," said Ada.

"As you say," said Peebs. "And a supposedly ancient fish at that! But with the acquisition tomorrow, and your grandmother's footmen covering all the exits, I cannot see a way around the matter."

"Here," said Ada, plucking an envelope from under her pillow and handing it to Peebs.

"What is this, Lady Ada?" he asked.

"A last resort," Ada answered. "Go to the acquisition, and swap this out with the letter Miss Anning wrote to authenticate the bones. And be clandestine."

"And this document here would be . . . ?"

"A forgery. A fake. Counterfeit. I copied Miss Anning's handwriting, pretending to be her. It says the

bones are as fake as this letter really is. Only this one tells the truth."

"Spurious!" said Anna proudly.

"A false letter that tells the truth, rather than a real letter that tells a lie," said Peebs. "Remarkable."

"Well, as I said, it is our last resort," said Ada. "Until I come up with a . . . um . . . first resort."

Peebs considered this for a moment and nodded. "I shall attend the acquisition tomorrow. This much I can promise."

Ada pretended she had stopped listening and submerged herself in her book. Peebs excused himself and left.

Ada waited ten full seconds, counting as slowly as she could, which wasn't very.

"Anna," said Ada intently. "Seamstresses."

LOT 221B

The morning of the acquisition, Mary, her stepsister (and sometime Wollstonecraft detective) Jane, and a wan-looking Charles arrived at the museum by carriage. They stepped out into the chilly drizzle onto the crunch of wet gravel, which was busy collecting small puddles in hopes of putting them together.

Under the portico of the old building was a damp Peebs, who doffed his hat to the girls and shook Charles's hand.

"I say, young Master Dickens, are you altogether well?" he asked.

"I . . . I skipped breakfast, is all, Mr. Shelley, but thank you for asking."

Jane and Mary looked nervously at one another, Jane's curls getting frizzier in the wet.

"Should we wait for Allegra?" asked Jane. "Is she coming?"

"Can she?" asked Mary.

"That is entirely up to Mrs. Woolcott now," said Peebs. "But the acquisition is starting soon."

"I wish Ada were here," said Mary. "I'm unsure of what to do."

"Lady Ada seems certain that once this envelope," said Peebs, holding it up, "is read in place of the real one, the Sons of Bavaria will show their hand. We must be ready."

"But we don't know what that means," protested Mary. "We don't know precisely what they will do, and we don't know what to do when they do it. It doesn't seem much of a plan."

"It does seem like poking a hornet's nest," added Jane. "How can we be sure that will help us recover the dog?"

"Ada does like an experiment," agreed Charles. "I think we must trust in her plan, and see it through."

There was quite a throng gathering outside, waiting for the doors to open and for the acquisition to begin. In fact, it was difficult to see, through the sea of hats and umbrellas, precisely who was in the crowd, though on occasion it was possible to make out a stand of bearded men with aprons, their sleeves rolled up like grocers'. One held a lidded wicker basket, slightly larger than a breadbox, as though he were about to make a grocery delivery or attend a picnic.

"Peebs," asked Jane, "is there any chance whatsoever of Ada making it out of the house?"

"I fear not, Miss Jane," said Peebs. "Lady Noel has every door well guarded."

"Every one she knows about, anyway," mused Mary. "The museum doors are opening. We should go in."

The crowd compressed itself through the doors and down the long, package-cramped hallway to the auditorium, where the acquisition was to take place. Many of the crates were under tarpaulins, like lumpy ghosts of camels and elephants. It created a landscape of uncertain forms, and so with each step Jane and Mary and Charles and Peebs entered uncertain territory.

There was quite the hubbub, given that it was a weekday, but all manner of onlookers were in attendance. Workmen, who had labored to load and unload the crates, and were curious as to their contents, rubbed shoulders with bored Society ladies with little else to amuse themselves. Journalists jostled enthusiasts of the natural sciences, and trod on the toes of plotting villains and intrepid detectives alike.

Ladies, both young and those of advanced years, had taken all the available seating, leaving a multitude of standing men and a lone woman in a distinctive straw hat at the far end of the hall.

Miss Anning.

Mary, standing on tiptoes, could make out the long tables of artifacts, each with a polished wooden document stand upon which was a sealed letter of authenticity for that item. Most artifacts were revealed, but there was a long rectangular case that was draped so as to conceal its contents. However, it was the only thing on the table large enough to be a dinosaur—even a fake one. Mary nodded to Peebs.

A gentleman looking very much like a judge was on the stage and banged a gavel with each new acquisition, its authenticity publicly verified and price agreed upon. They were nearly up to Lot 221B.

Peebs made his move, *excuse me*-ing through the throng. He had to get to the very visible document stand in front of the fake bones and switch the envelope there with the one in his breast pocket, without being seen. And he had only moments in which to do it. There were more pardons asked for than excuses made as he inadvertently trod on toes and hemlines alike in an effort to snake his way through.

He came face to face with a youngish woman in a large straw hat, who was clearly distraught. Peebs was moved by the sadness of her face when he realized this must be the famous paleontologist Mary Anning. He did not know what to say, and thought it best to remain silent while squeezing past and not stepping on her shoes.

His prize now in sight, Peebs slipped between a rather rotund gentleman and his exceedingly stringy wife, a mere three paces from the document stand. Suddenly stepping between Peebs and the red-draped table were three identically clad bearded men, in grocer's aprons, their sleeves rolled up.

The Sons of Bavaria!

Peebs pretended he was lost, looking left and right, trying to step through nonchalantly. But to no avail. The men gave him a shove, and Peebs fell backward awkwardly to the carpeted floor. There was a cracking sound, and he thought for a moment that he had broken himself, but then he realized that it was the bang of the gavel. The museum had read the documents on and formally purchased a ceramic comb from the Ming dynasty.

"Sir, allow me to assist you," said Mary, pretending to be a helpful stranger. He thanked her for her kindness, however unusual it appeared for a girl to help a gentleman to his feet. Peebs passed the envelope to Mary discreetly. The Sons of Bavaria were onto him: perhaps Mary would stand a better chance. Mary curtsied properly and briefly, and turned toward the target.

In doing so, she caught sight of Miss Anning, whose eyes practically bulged out a warning. Mary ignored it.

The Sons of Bavaria were still focused on Peebs, and Mary was able to slip around them with nary a word.

And there it was, in a glass-fronted box, like a very

large painting, only this painting was as deep as her forearm. Set into what, to Mary, was clearly plaster painted to look like dirt were odd, disconnected animal bones, assembled into some sort of fantastical shape of teeth and flippers. A cheaply made sea monster of ha'penny-a-peek exhibitions with no hope of convincing anybody of anything without the sworn word of a prominent scientist.

And of course the document in an envelope, in front of the ridiculously fake dinosaur bones, saying they were real, even though they were not. Mary took a step closer, envelope at the ready.

"'Ere for the spoon, then, miss?" asked the museum guard she'd met before. He had stepped directly in front of Mary, grinning broadly.

"Exciting, innit? Richard the Lion-Heart's very own spoon."

"Um, w-well, y-yes," stammered Mary. "Exciting."

"Cor, look at all these people. Lots to see, eh? Mind you, some real 'istory 'ere, what with your famous spoon and all."

Mary had no idea how to get around the enthusiastic guard. For the second time, she felt bad for the man; first for being subjected to what Ada does

152

to authority figures, and now for his impending disappointment. She was momentarily jostled from behind, and half turned to see who it was who brushed past her. A young man, tugging his cap in feigned apology.

"Pardon my clumsiness, miss." And that was Charles, who had relieved her of the envelope with the stealth of a pickpocket.

Mary watched Charles try to navigate the crush of onlookers, searching for a path to the document stand, only to run again and again into a wall of aproned, bearded, tattoo-less yet aspiring criminals.

As Charles's eyes swept the room, looking for other avenues, a young lady adjacent dropped her glove on the hall's floor. Smiling, he bent down to retrieve it for her, handing it back with a slight bow. Jane graciously received it, noticing that folded in the returned glove was the envelope.

Each step was a mile, a hundred miles in the crowd, despite the actual number of steps between Jane's envelope and the real one. Closer.

Closer. And yet not close enough.

Not by miles.

Mary heard several words from the podium: One

was "dinosaur." Another was "authenticate." And yet another was "now."

She saw a second guard lean in behind his chatty fellow and pluck the envelope—the original and entirely wrong envelope—from its stand and deliver it to the podium.

They had failed. Mary could scarcely believe it.

The judge-looking person cracked the seal and said something with regard to Lot 221B, the Cretaceous ichthyosaurus.

Among the new set of words was "fake." And "counterfeit." And "spurious."

Jane reached Mary and handed over the other envelope out of desperation and confusion. Mary then double-checked the envelope in her hand, the one bearing the note forged by Ada, declaring the bones to be precisely what the judge-looking person had just told the assembled they were.

Impossibly, both notes said the same thing. The bones were forgeries, the sellers frauds.

The shock of scandal swept the room. Mary turned to Miss Anning, resolute and sorrowful. Despite her own desire to see her beloved dog restored to her, she had told the truth, no matter the cost to her own feelings, and the fate of poor Tray the terrier.

"I say!" said the formerly enthusiastic guard. "The cheek!" He joined the other guards to contain the crowd, which pushed to see the now-revealed-to-be-fake bones.

Mary also had to admit that Ada was right. The Sons of Bavaria were making their move—a fast move for the exit. Mary felt Peebs take her elbow, and they rushed, as best they could in the crush of the crowd, after them, with Charles and Jane just behind them. A whistle blew. Mary looked back to see Miss Anning speaking to two guards and pointing at the bearded, aproned, rolled-sleeved, and tattoo-less men.

The doors flew open. With little regard for courtesy, Mary and Peebs managed to get out to the open cobblestone courtyard that led to the green. Seven of the Sons of Bavaria, including one with a picnic basket, ran north toward the wood of Russell Square.

Getting away.

PETRICHOR

Suddenly one of the villains dropped to the cobbles, pinned like a butterfly to a card. There was a burlap sack the size of a pillowcase next to him, and sand seeped from a split in the cloth. The man was out cold.

Mary looked up. A familiar-looking and positively Brobdingnagian wicker basket, the largest she had ever seen, was descending from the sky, beneath an enormous striped balloon. Steam and smoke and soot spat from the gleaming brass steam engine that chuffed from the basket's center. And peeking over the top were two small girls.

With her penknife, Allegra snicked the rope of another sandbag, sending it plunging into the courtyard. Down went another of the bearded grocers with a wince-inducing *bap!*

"Ha-ha!" Allegra cried. "Keep it steady, Ada! We've got them lined up!" she roared over the sound of wind. *Snick* went another rope, and *thud* went another of the apron-clad scoundrels.

Mary waved up to a beaming Ada, who seemed to have sprouted another hand, she was so busy working the controls of the engine and the ropes of the balloon all at once. This left Allegra to bomb the Sons of Bavaria with sandbags, and she was getting quite good at it.

At last, there was only one crook left standing, the one with the picnic basket. The wind seemed not to be cooperating, and as the balloon had risen somewhat with each dropped sandbag, Ada struggled to send the whole works in the right direction in pursuit.

Mary had an idea, though she admitted to herself it was not an honest one.

She found the previously chatty guard and shouted, "He's got the spoon! He's getting away!"

"Richard the Lion-Heart's spoon!" said the enthusiastic guard, as a battle cry. With tremendous vigor
and a bravery fueled by patriotism and the defense of
history, the guard raced toward, and finally tackled,
the last of the Sons of Bavaria.

The crowd applauded. The picnic basket the man
had been carrying tumbled, and from within could

be heard a muffled yapping, and then a proper bark.
The basket's lid gave way, and out popped a small,
rectangular, and bushy-browed terrier.

"Tray!" exclaimed Miss Anning, emerging from
the gaggle of onlookers. Barking happily all the way,
the little dog ran to the brilliant, honest, and he-
roic paleontologist, leaping into her arms. The sight

warmed Mary's heart. Peebs went over, to be sure Miss Anning was all right.

The balloon landed, and a rope ladder was thrown out. As Allegra descended, she was met by the impressed crowd with applause and was hoisted onto the shoulders of several men who waved their hats in triumph.

She was followed by a rather sooty and disheveled Ada, who, when others came to put her on their shoulders, shooed them away. She ran instead to Mary.

"We did it!" she cried.

"We didn't," Mary admitted. "We didn't make the switch in time."

"Oh, that's all right," said Ada. "I knew Miss Anning would tell the truth, and the Sons of Bavaria would go running. We just had to be there to intercept them when they did."

"But," started Mary. "She rejected your plan!"

"No, Miss Anning never read my plan. It never even got to her. The letter I received was a forgery. A joke, really. Took me a while to get it, though."

"A joke?" Mary asked in astonishment.

"Yes, look." Ada presented the crumpled note from

the pocket of her dress. "Heraldry. You know, crests and shields of medieval knights. It's a golden alder."

"Miss Anning was staying at the Golden Alder Inn."

"Yes, but in heraldry the colors are spelled out in French. So this crest would be 'an alder or,' meaning 'gold.'"

"So?" asked Jane.

"An alder or! Learn Road! Adorn Earl!" Ada answered excitedly.

"Nora Radel," said Mary, realizing. "You were right! She was behind it all along. The cleverest girl in England."

"Second cleverest, if you ask me," said Ada. "And no, not exactly behind it. I think there was a real dognapping and perhaps she suggested the fakery. Mostly I think she saw a way of putting herself in the middle, and confusing the whole works."

"But . . . why?" asked Jane. "Why would she do that?"

"It's a challenge," said Ada. "A challenge I accepted."

"However do you know that?" Peebs asked, joining them.

"I'll explain later. Right now we have to get back before Gran knows I'm gone."

"How did you manage to effect an escape, Lady Ada?" Peebs asked. "Your grandmother was watching every door."

"She wasn't watching the roof," Ada answered, grinning. "The steam engine works brilliantly, Peebs, thank you."

"But how . . . ?" Mary wanted to know.

"Seamstresses. I've had Anna on them for weeks. Along with riggers, and pipe fitters. And when I saw that marvelous basket the other day, full of cotton, I knew I'd found my new gondola. Mr. Franklin has proved most helpful with the logistics."

Allegra was still enjoying being carried by the cheering assembly. Ada rolled her eyes.

"But who were the tick-tock people?" Mary asked. "And how did they get into the house, when your grandmother was watching all the doors?"

"I don't know yet why they look that way, but I know they work for *her,*" said Ada, meaning Nora Radel and not her grandmother. "And they must have someone on the inside," she added ominously. "But we shall deal with that when we get home. All in! And someone fetch my sister."

Ada stepped away to approach a very appreciative Miss Anning, clutching her little dog to her chest, the terrier's tongue happily lapping the tears from the scientist's cheek. Ada nodded, and received a nod in return.

The rain had ceased, briefly, though for a London in December it was never more than a moment's reprieve. Ada breathed in the scent of the earth and discovered that Miss Anning was doing the same.

"Petrichor," said Miss Anning. "The smell of earth after rain."

Ada smiled.

COPROLITE

Oh, how Ada had missed the familiar sensation of swinging from rope to roof to attic windowsill. The rest of her party were less rehearsed, and the roof was slick with rain. But one by one, and with many utterings of "steady, steady," they all made it through to stand in the long, sparse room, dripping on the floorboards.

"Ah, I've just remembered," said Peebs. "I have something for you, a token. From Miss Anning." From his pocket he brought forth a handkerchief wrapped around a small object and handed it to Ada. Inside was a ridged brown stone, pointy at one end.

"A rock?" asked Jane.

"A coprolite!" exclaimed Ada, holding it up in the thin attic light. "It's magnificent!"

"What's that?" Allegra asked, not even trying to pronounce it.

"It's poo! Real dinosaur poo!" Ada explained delightedly. "Only, turned to stone! Isn't it amazing?"

Allegra, Mary, and Jane all made the same face. Charles tried not to laugh.

"Happy birthday, Lady Ada," said Peebs.

"Is it?" Ada asked. "What's the date?"

"The tenth of December, Lady Ada," Peebs answered.

"Gosh, I'd forgotten. It really is my birthday," she said.

The girls, surprised, all wished her a happy birthday as a chorus, and Ada shushed them, so as not to make so much noise that they would be discovered.

"I'm twelve," said Ada.

"That's ancient," said nine-year-old Allegra. "Old as dinosaur poo."

They all had a good laugh at this, and Jane tried, unsuccessfully, to seem offended.

"Master Dickens," interrupted Peebs, seizing the moment. "I understand that you are in need of employment."

"I am, sir," he answered.

"And that you've recently proved yourself extremely resourceful in the matter of research, and church records?"

"And in the archives of the *Times,*" added Mary. "For our first case. We'd be nowhere without Charles, honestly."

Peebs strode toward a small writing desk in the corner of the room, took a sheet of paper and a quill, and began scribbling. The attic's inkpot, though more dry than ideal, proved serviceable enough.

"If you would take . . . this . . . note . . . ," he said, "to my attorneys at the firm of Ellis and Blackmore, Holborn Court, Grey's Inn—do you know it?"

"I do, Mr. Shelley, sir."

"Very good. Take them this letter of introduction, and make yourself useful. I imagine you'll find it rather less . . . um . . . than the boot-polish factory."

"I have little cause to doubt your imagination, Mr. Shelley."

"Excellent. And, in this house, you must call me Peebs."

Charles smiled. "Peebs."

Ada gave Peebs an approving nod.

"Ada, may I have a word?" Jane asked.

They took a few discreet steps away from the others.

"I'm sorry," Jane said.

"For what?" Ada was confused.

"For being horrid, I suppose," Jane began. "It's like this. When it was just my mother and I, we were very poor. And it wasn't until she met Mr. Godwin that we had any real home to speak of, and a family. I always dreamt of being in a grand house, and of entering Society." Ada nodded, though she wasn't sure why she was doing that.

"When the chance came to meet you, and to study at your home, I felt, after wishing so long, that it was something I was supposed to have. Something I deserved. And I was a ghastly snob, I must admit it."

"A little bit," agreed Ada, factually.

"And then after our last case, when I saw how awful Society could be, and how unfair, it rather broke my heart."

"I told Mary we broke you," Ada said.

"Not you, and that's the point."

"Oh?" said Ada, not really understanding at all.

"What I mean to say is, I care not a whit for Society anymore," said Jane. "But I do want to help, and I want very much to be your friend."

And with that Jane threw her arms around Ada, which made her go quite stiff, although she didn't mind as much as she thought she might.

Ada nodded and pointed at the others. The two girls rejoined the group.

"Are you all right, Ada?" asked Mary quietly.

"Bit hugged is all," said Ada. "Now we all have to sneak out of here."

"Not all," said Peebs. "You must return to your room, Lady Ada. As for Master Dickens and myself, well, I am a familiar face and may go as I please, even if my arrival is sometimes suspect. Master Dickens shall carry my valise, and none shall be the wiser. We will depart from the front. Mary, if you take the girls down the servants' stairs, I imagine that is your best bet."

"I'll come down too," said Ada. "I won't get in too much trouble if I'm just coming down for bread and butter."

"You're covered in soot," said Jane.

"And you're wet," said Allegra. Ada just shrugged.

The gentlemen went first, as an advance guard, with an agreed-upon signal of coughing awkwardly should the halls be full of Gran's footmen. Hearing nothing, the girls descended the attic stairs and then went down the hall to the servants' staircase.

Ada led the way, having the least to lose if discovered. But the coast was momentarily clear, and Ada, then Mary, then Jane, then Allegra filed into the upstairs kitchen and headed for the back door to the garden. After some shushing and silent smiles, Mary placed her hand on the doorknob.

A squeak from the stairway to the servants' floor halted them, and they turned in unison.

There framed in the doorway stood Mrs. Chowser, although a very transformed Mrs. Chowser. Her face was painted with white powder, and round red circles were drawn upon her cheeks. Lines of greasepaint had been inscribed upon her wrists and every joint of her fingers, and one ugly-looking line ran across

her throat, like her head could be popped off at any moment.

But what alarmed Ada the most was a fresh, angry-looking tattoo upon the cook's right inner forearm: the letters *S O B Q J M V,* inscribed upon Mrs. Chowser's still-stinging skin.

"Tick," said the puppet–Mrs. Chowser. "Tock."

AGHAST

The Wollstonecraft girls stood aghast.

Ada was certain that the tick-tock puppet couple had been working for Nora Radel, and here was another of her accomplices. But to find that her latest accomplice was a trusted member of Ada's own household . . . Ada felt some shame in only just having remembered the woman's name after so many years, but such guilt was diminished by the cook's obvious betrayal.

Suddenly it all made sense. It was Mrs. Chowser who had kept Ada's mother informed of the goings-on at the Marylebone house. It was she who had betrayed the presence and real identity of Peebs, when he first arrived under a clandestine name. And it was Mrs. Chowser who had allowed the entry of the tick-tock pair into the parlor for the attempted dognapping of Charlemagne.

Ada turned to the other girls, who were clearly frightened by Mrs. Chowser's comical yet nightmarish appearance. Ada leaned closer to her (former, she supposed) cook, to see the details of the greasepaint, and of the painful-looking tattoo.

The look in Mrs. Chowser's eyes was distant and unfocused. As though she were dreaming. As though, in fact, she were under some kind of uncanny influence.

Uncanny influence. Mesmerism.

Ada reached out curiously, slowly, carefully, and snapped her fingers.

Nothing. Mrs. Chowser's expression remained expressionless.

"Tick," said the cook again.

"Tock," came a voice behind the girls. Two voices, in fact.

They all turned completely around to face the door

to the kitchen garden. It was now flanked by two of Gran's footmen, both painted as dolls to match Mrs. Chowser, and both with the identical distant expression.

Jane shrieked in horror.

"Up!" shouted Ada, pointing at the stairs. As the gaggle of girls reversed their course and went back up the servants' stairway, Ada remembered something. She darted back down, between the two approaching footmen, who were lurching oddly as though sleepwalking, and bolted to the distillery closet. She knew precisely what she was looking for, so it took her only a heartbeat to locate it and snatch it off the shelf. Holding a small jar of white powder, she again wove between the doll-painted footmen and tore up the stairs after her friends.

Allegra was first at the top, and almost matched Jane's scream when she came face to face with Anna.

Allegra scanned the maid's countenance for any change, but there was no paint upon her face, no disconcerting lines around her joints, and no fresh tattoo upon her arm. Just a look of concern, no doubt instigated by Jane's outburst downstairs. Behind Anna loomed a perfectly ordinary-looking (for him)

Mr. Franklin. The girls all piled up on the landing in the hallway, the footmen and Mrs. Chowser in pursuit.

Looking over the railing, Ada could see the original puppet-couple standing by the open front door, making their way toward the stairs.

"Room!" shouted Ada, scrambling past the other girls with her prized jar. They all followed, grateful for Mr. Franklin's protective immensity guarding the rear.

The six of them poured into Ada's bedroom and latched the door.

"Lady Ada?" asked a frightened Anna. "Whatever is going on?"

"Puppets! Mesmerism! Uncanny influence!" Ada panted. "It's marvelous, and it explains everything! It was never the acorn necklace—the one that could supposedly mesmerize people from our first case, you remember. It never made sense! I can finally take it out of the intractables book! Nora Radel must have some *other* way to mesmerize people. Though—maybe how *she* does it should go back in the intractables book."

"Ada!" Mary brought the excited girl back to the present moment.

"Sorry, it's just tremendously interesting," Ada apologized.

"And scary! They're everywhere!" shouted Allegra.

"Ada?" asked Mary. "What are we to do?"

Ada glanced about the room, and then seemed to notice the jar in her hand.

"Ah," she said quite casually. "Bomb."

"You said you were making muffins, Lady Ada," noted Anna.

"Lied," said Ada, hauling the cast-iron pot from beneath her bed. As she righted the concoction, they could all see the large wrench embedded in the brown sugary cement. Ada struggled with the jar lid for a moment and then handed the thing over her shoulder without looking. Elegantly Mr. Franklin stepped around the girls, took the jar from Ada's hand, effortlessly opened the lid, and handed the jar back to Ada, who sprinkled the shimmering white contents on top of the brown goo.

"You can't set off a bomb in the house, Lady Ada!" said Anna. "You'll burn down the whole place!"

"That's what we want them to think," said Ada.

"Ada," said Mary, attempting to remain calm. "We

trust you. We shall do as you say. But please do tell us the plan, and please do tell us it does not involve burning down the house."

"Uncanny influence. Mesmerism. We've seen it before," said Ada.

Mary nodded. They hadn't actually seen it, but they'd been aware of it, from their first case.

"Right, well," Ada continued. "This will either shock them out of it or at least get them out of the house, and give us time to think. Match," she asked of Mr. Franklin.

"Ada," Jane said. "That's a bomb. Bombs explode. You can't light that in here."

"Counterfeit," said Ada. "Counterfeit bones, counterfeit letters, a counterfeit case, with counterfeit clues. Counterfeit criminals—or real criminals with counterfeit cleverness—and counterfeit dolls. This," she said, smiling, "is a counterfeit bomb. Match!" she demanded, and Anna handed her one from the fireplace box.

"Now," said Ada, hauling the pot to her door, "Mr. Franklin, when I give the signal, you open the door."

"But there are scary people ticking and tocking out there," said Allegra nervously.

"Not for long," said Ada. "Everybody, close your eyes. On three. One. Two. Three!"

With that, Mr. Franklin opened the door, and Ada struck the match. Even through their closed eyes, they could all see that the flash of the flame meeting the magnesium powder on top of the counterfeit bomb was brilliant, and would momentarily blind anyone who looked at it unprepared. As they all blinked and their eyes adjusted, they could see a thick black smoke pouring out of the pot and roiling down the hallway, almost like a syrup.

"Fire!" shouted Ada. "Fire, fire, fire!" And with this cry she tipped the pot on its side and rolled it toward the main stairs, where it bounced and continued to spew a choking black billow of smoke in all directions, the wrench thudding menacingly as it went.

At first, the tick-tock people did nothing, but after a brief pause they looked at one another and panicked.

"Fire!" they shouted, as though they had awoken from a dream only to find themselves in a nightmare, surrounded by strangely painted people and a house on fire. "Fire!"

Ada could barely see through the smoke but could

make out a footman ushering her grandmother through the open door, a yapping Charlemagne tucked safely under her arm.

Coughing, Ada shut the door after the household, painted or otherwise, fled the building. Only the four girls, Anna, and Mr. Franklin remained. Anna had opened the flue for air as Mr. Franklin worked at the stubborn windows.

"All smoke, no fire. Counterfeit bomb," said Ada, pleased with herself.

"And you kept that under the bed?" asked Jane.

"Well, I was going to use it before. To sneak out of the house. But Mary had a better idea."

Allegra was still absorbing the idea that Ada had been sleeping with a bomb under her bed, just in case.

"Where did they come from?" asked Jane.

"Nora Radel," answered Ada. "The so-called cleverest girl in England. Criminal mastermind and my archnemesis. She got in the middle of our case somehow and, using what I can only assume to be some kind of mesmerism, makes people dress like puppets and do her bidding. Quite practical, really."

"But Mrs. Chowser," said Allegra.

"Yes," said Ada. "It was Mrs. Chowser the cook

who was the spy in our house. Well, when it wasn't Peebs. But he was the right sort of spy."

Allegra looked confused.

"Anyway," Ada continued, "seeing that Mrs. Chowser was not exactly loyal, Nora Radel found a way to get to her. And no doubt that was the least she was up to. I think she helps not-so-clever criminals, like the ones we've encountered, by giving them ideas, information. And if she helps them a lot, in return she makes them wear her mark."

"The tattoo?" asked Jane. "Whatever does it mean?"

"*S O B Q J M V.* It's her name, the Sphinx of Black Quartz. It's not the Sons of Bavaria at all, though the hunch got me on the right track," said Ada, exchanging nods with Mary. "That's why I signed the note I left at the museum using her name. So they'd be confused and contact her, which would force her hand. And it worked, so she sent the doll people to kidnap Charlemagne, to be safe. I couldn't sort out her plan, but I could make it untidy for her."

"Sphinx of Black Quartz? But why such an unusual—" Jane began.

"She loves word games, clearly," Ada explained.

"It's a famous pangram. Sphinx of Black Quartz Judge My Vow." She looked around the room at blank expressions. "A pangram is a phrase containing every letter of the alphabet, like 'Heavy boxes perform quick waltzes and jigs.' They're good fun."

"A game?" said Jane. "A cruel game."

Just then, there was an unexpected knock on the door.

"Lady Ada? Miss Mary? Are you all right?"

Peebs.

Mr. Franklin opened the door, and in the still-smoky-but-clearing hallway stood Peebs, hat in hand. Peebs looked around the room at its harried occupants.

"I've locked up the house, front and back. We should all be perfectly safe for the time being," he said.

"However did you know?" asked Mary.

"I heard the fire brigade as I was walking home, and thought it awfully close to here. So I returned out of concern."

"The fire brigade!" Jane exclaimed. "I hope they don't drown the place!"

"Oh, I've sent them home," said Peebs. "It may surprise you that I was a boy once, and I know a classic saltpeter-and-sugar smoke bomb when I see one. Whatever was that in aid of, if I may ask?"

"Minions," Ada answered. "Evil minions."

"And the banishment thereof," concluded Mary.

"Well, it seems to have worked, even if you include your grandmother amongst them. I saw her carriage flee the scene with some haste."

"She'll be back," said Ada.

"I suspect they'll all be back," said Jane. "Good and wicked, in due course."

"Well, for now," said Anna, "I'm grateful we're all safe."

"And together," said Mary, reaching out for Ada's hand.

"Ada?" said Allegra, gripping Ada's other hand. "Happy birthday."

NOTES

1826

The year itself is practically a character in this series. John Quincy Adams was president of the United States. The prince regent of England had become King George IV just six years before, and the future Queen Victoria was only seven years old. By 1826, the world had seen a recent flurry of inventions: Volta's electric battery (1800), Fulton's submarine and torpedo (1800), Winsor's patented gas lighting (1804), Trevithick's steam locomotive (1804), Davy's electric arc light (1809), Bell's steam-powered boat (1812), and Sturgeon's electromagnet (1824). It was an exciting time of technological advancement, and it brought forth two very bright girls who changed the world through their intellect and imagination.

The lives of women—and particularly girls—were extremely limited and under constant watch. Women were not allowed to vote or practice professions, and were widely thought to be less capable than men. A girl's value to her family was in her reputation and her service, and she was expected to obediently accept a husband of her parents' choosing. Any threat to that reputation—like behaving unusually—was often enough to ruin a family.

However, because girls were not expected to have a career and compete with their (or anybody's) husband, upper-class girls were free to read or study as they wished, for few took them seriously. Because of this rare freedom, the nineteenth century saw a sharp

ADA

surge in the intellectual contributions of female scientists and mathematicians, with Ada foremost among them.

AUGUSTA ADA BYRON (1815–1852) was a brilliant mathematician and the daughter of the poet Lord Byron (who died when Ada was eight). Largely abandoned by her mother, she was raised by servants (and sometimes her grandmother) at the Marylebone house and was very much cut off from the world as a child.

With her legendary temper and lack of social skills (a modern historian unkindly calls her "mad as a hatter"), Ada made few friends. Her mother insisted that young Ada have no connection to her father's friends or even his interests, so Ada turned to mathematics. She worked with her friend Charles Babbage on the tables of numbers for Babbage's "Analytical Engine"—a mechanical computer—which was not built in his lifetime. But Ada's contribution to the work, as well as her idea that computers could be used not only for mathematics but also for creative works such as music, has caused many people to refer to Ada as "the world's first computer programmer." Babbage called her the Enchantress of Numbers.

Ada grew to control her temper and insecurities, and was married at nineteen to William King, a baron, who became the Count of Lovelace three years later. This is why Ada is more commonly known as Ada Lovelace. She had three children—Byron, Annabella, and Ralph—and died of cancer at the age of thirty-six. She continues to inspire scientists and mathematicians to this day, and many worthwhile projects are named after her.

MARY WOLLSTONECRAFT GOD~ WIN (1797–1851) was the daughter of the famous feminist writer Mary Wollstonecraft (who died ten days after giving birth) and the political philosopher William Godwin. William Godwin married Mary Jane Clairmont in 1801, and Mary grew up in a mixed household of half siblings and stepsiblings in Somers Town, in northern London. She read broadly and had an appetite for adventure and romanticism. She ran away with Percy Shelley at age sixteen, and over one very famous weekend with Shelley, Lord Byron (Ada's father), and early vampire novelist Dr. John Polidori, Mary came up with the idea for the world's first science-fiction novel—*Frankenstein; or, The Modern Prometheus*—which she wrote at age nineteen.

In real life, Mary was eighteen years older than Ada. But I thought it would be more fun this way—to cast these two luminaries as friends.

PERCY BYSSHE (rhymes with "fish") SHELLEY (1792–1822) was an important poet and best friend to Ada's father, Lord Byron. Percy came from a wealthy family, and he offered to support Mary's father and the Godwin family. At age twenty-two, he ran off with then-sixteen-year-old Mary to Switzerland, and they were married two years later. He drowned at the age of twenty-nine when his sailboat sank in a storm.

While in reality, Peebs had died even before our story begins, I have extended his life so that they can be in this story together. It is Peebs, as Ada's father's friend and Mary's future husband, who provides a real-life link between our two heroines.

CHARLES DICKENS (1812–1870) is considered one of the great writers of Victorian England. He really was fourteen in 1826, and he really did work in a boot-polish factory gluing labels. He would later work for the law firm of Ellis and Blackmore—though not because of a referral from Peebs! He loved books and was a keen observer of everyday life in London. He is perhaps best known to young readers as the author of *A Christmas Carol*.

CLARA ("CLAIRE") MARY JANE CLAIRMONT (1798–1879) was known as Jane as a child but later adopted the name Claire. She really was Mary's stepsister (her mother married Mary's father), but her real life diverges dramatically from this story. Jane was actually Allegra's mother! I adjusted her timeline and role so that the two sets of sisters—Ada and Allegra, Mary and Jane—could work together as friends and detectives.

Lord Byron called Claire "a little fiend," but she referred to him as a few moments of happiness and a lifetime of trouble. She was an aspiring novelist and extremely well-read. Claire traveled throughout Europe, living in Russia for a time, returning to England to care for her mother, moving to Paris, and then finally settling in Italy. She was the longest-lived of all the Shelley-Byron circle.

ALLEGRA

CLARA ALLEGRA (ALBA) BYRON (1817–1822) was the daughter of Claire Clairmont and Lord Byron. Her mother could not care for her, so she was left with her father. He, however, frequently left her in the care of strangers, eventually placing her in a convent in Italy. She died of fever at the age of five, but I have moved her timeline and brought her to life in the world of Wollstonecraft, to be a truer sister to Ada.

MARY ANNING (1799–1847) was an early paleontologist credited with discovering the first ichthyosaur skeleton. Dinosaur hunting being something of a family business, she found her first skull at the age of eleven, and also contributed to the identification of coprolites, the fossilized dinosaur poo she gifts Ada as a birthday present. Her work was supported by sales of prints of the illustration made by her friend Henry De la Beche depicting the ancient Dorset revealed by the fossil discoveries Mary made. She really did have a dog, Tray, lost in a landslide that occurred while she was fossil hunting. Despite her obvious accomplishments and significant contributions to her field of research, she was not allowed to join the Geological Society of London because she was a woman.

JOHN WILLIAM POLIDORI (1795–1821) was a physician,

poet, and horror writer who is credited with writing the first vampire story in English. He was a good friend of both Lord Byron and Percy Shelley. As he was dead before our story takes place, his timeline has been adjusted to mesh with that of Peebs, Jane, and Mary. Because of the era's use of leeches in medicine, I have made him a bit of a vampire himself. He was an Englishman, despite his Italian name, and had no "unplaceable" accent. His eyebrows, however, were entirely terrifying.

THE BRITISH MUSEUM Established in 1753 and under constant expansion for its first hundred years, the British Museum became the model of scientific and historical museums around the world. Particularly during the events of this book, it was the largest construction site in Europe, and Ada most certainly would have heard the hammering and clamor from her rooftop perch in Marylebone.

Join the Wollstonecraft Detectives on their next case!
Here's a sneak peek of their next mystery—
a case brought to them by royal request . . .

PETULANT

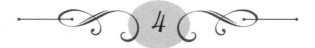

Ada, at the upward-shushing hand of her grand-mother, got up from the couch as the Baroness Lehzen rose to go.

Gran remained in the doorway, still not sure if she should be pleased, or proud, or horrified.

"Well?" Gran asked once Mr. Franklin had seen out their auspicious guest.

"'Well' what?" Ada replied.

"You failed to indicate to the baroness that you would of course offer your assistance in her confidential matter, though I must say she does play her cards close, that one."

"She wasn't playing cards," said Ada, distantly. She was reviewing her last conversation, unsure if she had all the important bits. Unsure if she had any bits, really.

The baroness had turned out to be so well-mannered and polite that she barely seemed to say anything at all. And with Gran haunting the doorframe like that, constantly gesturing for Ada to smooth her gown or improve her posture, Ada was unable to concentrate on what had in fact been said, if anything.

"Surely," Gran tried again, "you could have made your offer of assistance plain."

"No."

"Good heavens, child. What on earth do you mean by 'no' in this instance? It is inconceivable."

"Isn't. I can conceive of it. No. Not helping," came Ada's terse reply.

"Of course you are helping. Why ever would you not?"

"You," said Ada. "Because of you."

"Young Ada, now is not the time to be petulant." Gran looked at the sulking girl across the room and explained, " 'Petulant' means—"

"Insolent. Irritable. Uncooperative. From the Latin *petulans,* meaning impudent." Ada's eyebrows were a threat.

"Very well, then," said Gran. "Have you any idea to whom you were just speaking? Why, even your cousin Medora Leigh—"

"Medora?" Ada asked.

"Libby," Gran said with disdain.

"Ah," said Ada.

"Medora has attended the princess, many times I've heard." Gran sniffed. "From *that* side of the family. But you, Ada. Did you think how beneficial such a relationship might be to your family, to our standing?"

Ada didn't think her grandmother needed to be standing. In fact, she rather wished the old woman would sit down.

"That," Gran persevered, "was the Baroness Johanna Clara Louise Lehzen, governess to Her Royal Highness the Princess Alexandrina Victoria."

"I have no idea who that is. They is. Are. And even less of an idea of what they want. But I do know you want me to help, and that means I won't."

"You have no choice in the matter, girl. On that I must insist."

"You insist?" Ada began. "You forbid it just this morning."

"Pish," said Gran, flapping a handkerchief that seemed to have magically appeared for the purposes of flapping.

"'Unsuitable,' you said."

"But this is different," Gran protested. "This is *royalty.*"

"You have driven all my friends away—"

Gran flapped her handkerchief some more.

"—and you murdered my balloon, twenty-eight minutes ago."

"That contraption?" Gran's voice rose. "It heralded your demise, child, or worse—scandal. It is my duty to protect you and this family from the latter, at least, if it is within my power to do so. I shall not regret the execution of my duties."

"You shall regret the execution of my balloon," said Ada through gritted teeth. "And don't *pish* me," she added, because she was sure Gran was about to.

"All right," said Gran, crossing the room and finally taking a seat. "What do you want?"

A terrible shadow crossed Ada's face, full of purpose and quiet rage. "I want my balloon back."

"Impossible," answered Gran. And it was impossible. Even if Ada had an accurate weight of the steam engine and the coal and the balloon itself and the temperature of the air inside it, she still wouldn't know the wind direction or altitude of possible air currents. She had no way of knowing which way her balloon might possibly have blown, except vaguely north. Ish. Yes, Ada, acknowledged. Actually impossible.

"Then I want Mary back. And Peebs and Anna and everybody."

"Ada, you are to be in the presence of the princess. Your Mary is hardly of suitable breeding—"

"She is not a horse. She is my friend. And without her I can't help your baroness," said Ada, her frustration growing. "I can't help anybody."

Gran found Ada's frustration contagious. "Oh, honestly—"

"Bell rope," Ada said, and pointed.

Gran was taken aback. "What on earth—"

"Bell rope," Ada repeated. "Inside the walls of this house is a . . ." Ada laced her fingers together. "A lattice, a network of cables and pulleys. You pull the rope, the cable moves, and it rings a bell on a board below the stairs, in the servants' hall."

Gran blinked, attempting to understand.

"You've cut the bell ropes. I can do the bits in the walls, the tricky bits, that get results. But there's no velvet rope to pull. That's Mary. Nobody else wants to stick their arm in a spooky hole in the wall. I don't mind, but everyone else seems to. No, they want a rope. A nice, soft velvet rope, and Mary is the softest rope in the world."

Gran gave Ada a moment to compose herself.

"Very well," Gran answered. "I shall call for the return of your . . . compatriots. But are you certain about the maid? I can't abide—"

"Anna, too," Ada insisted.

"Very well," repeated Gran.

"And you go," said Ada, with an edge of cruelty she herself didn't like.

"Go?"

"You murdered my balloon. I want you to go away. Then I'll speak to your princess."

"She is very much your princess as well, Ada," Gran said softly. "And I shall reluctantly concede. Upon the completion of your assistance to Her Highness, and to Baroness Lehzen, I shall withdraw to Kirkby Mallory." Gran paused. "And your mother may do with you as she will."

Gran rose to leave, and offered a final word.

"Savor this victory, child, for no doubt its flavor shall turn to bitterness soon enough."

Over Gran's shoulder, a small pug could be seen, cheerfully scooching its bottom along the carpet.